For my [...]

Place of
Sage

Always listen
with you heart.
- You Place of Sage
friend,
Lyn D. Nielsen

Place of Sage

LYN D. NIELSEN

Pleasant Word
A Division of WINEPRESS PUBLISHING

Packaged by Pleasant Word, PO Box 428, Enumclaw, WA 98022. The views expressed or implied in this work do not necessarily reflect those of Pleasant Word. The author(s) is ultimately responsible for the design, content and editorial accuracy of this work.

Author photo by Maegan N. Kazas

ISBN 1-4141-0374-3
Library of Congress Catalog Card Number: 2005900501

For the First author and creator of *Place of Sage*, and for Dan . . . he'll see why.

Acknowledgements

This story began in 1996, has taken many years to complete, and is a journey that has altered not only my life, but others as well. As a result, I have many to thank . . . .

Dan, Maegan, and Keith—you walked a long, rough road with me, and I know your shoes are worn. Thank you for not giving up.

Jack and Joanne McLaren—Dad and Mom, you taught me the good things, and instilled a will to see things through, no matter how difficult. And because of your example, I know it's always worth it.

Nancy Coté—what would I do without you? You've gone beyond a sister's duty, and if you had a dollar for every time I asked, "May I run something by you?" you'd surely be in Hawaii by now.

Acknowledgements

Mike and Steve McLaren—my cool brothers, and good thing you are, or you'd never get away with calling me a "hermit."

Karen Straight—Aunt Karen, you encouraged me more than you know.

Brooke Turner—for permission to share your beautiful song.

Deanna Brown and Jen Moore—for that sparkle in your eyes, and your willingness to be part of something larger than us all. You on fire! (And it's not a typo.)

Vicky McNamara—for the frankincense, and reminding me about God's perfect timing—always when I needed it most.

Clyde A. Small ll—you're a good writer and friend, even though you hated me after reading *Place of Sage*, and told my skunk story to all of Grant County.

ShirleyRae Maes—for loaning me the entire *News & Standard* archives, and for the chicken soup.

Kay Dirks, Kathy Treiber, and Donna Huesties at the Ephrata Public Library—for research assistance, and letting me set up camp in the genealogy room.

Nancy Miller at the Coulee City Public Library—for your willingness to help.

Ann Sharley-Hubbard—for letting me tag along. You are one fine archaeologist.

Tim Brooks, Sr.; David Deieso and Floyd Jess—for teaching me ways of the land, and putting up with many questions.

Marvin Levy at DreamWorks, SKG—for your help, and great laugh.

Steven Spielberg—for allowing me to share a real moment from your life.

Karen at Sunny Delight—for helping me with research.

Marie at Shadowpoetry.com—for reprint permission, and your quick response.

Susan Johnson at Grant County PUD—for helping me understand Whale Island.

All my great friends—even though years went by, your excitement and prayers continued. You have no idea how much that helped.

Those who bought many copies of *Place of Sage* before it was even a book—what faith! I am grateful and humbled.

And finally, and foremost . . . .

The First author of this story—for not quitting on me, and for the many ways you show you're here.

Thank you everyone!

Preface

Sometimes, something big comes along and takes our life by surprise . . . so it has been with *Place of Sage*.

I can't take the credit for this story; so I'd like to tell you about the author who should.

He designed four-hundred-foot-high basalt walls to encompass the land called Place of Sage, and He flavored His setting with contrasts. For ruggedness, He gave it jagged rocks that change hues like a chameleon, deserted homesteads, bones bleached white in the sun, and tumbleweeds that bounce along the desert floor. And for a softness that leaves even writers wordless, He paints sunsets of purple—the kind where you blink to make sure they're real.

To illustrate the spirit here, a red-tailed hawk uses its whole body to push through a dust storm; resilient flowers, perfect in every detail, bloom unseen by human eyes; winds crescendo through the coulee like an ocean, or filter through like a flute; and to the sage He gave four seasons, each adorned in colors and perfume.

In this part of the desert, a coulee is known as, a canyon formed by ice age floods, but now considered dry. And since every great setting needs a feature, or two, of surprise, He poured an underground river beneath Place of Sage. Then He used the floods to shape a mesa resembling a six-story Aussie hat, placed it midstream in the coulee, and carved only one path to the top. The way is narrow, rocky, and steep; but He promised it's worth the climb.

It's the kind of place where . . . .

When you feel alone, and far from Him . . . He covers the mesa in fog, demonstrating that just because you can't see it, that doesn't mean it's not there.

When you are afraid . . . He stops a rattlesnake from biting your hand. And then to show His ways, He points out the mule deer; how they amble down from the top of the wall, in single file, brushing sage as they descend; and the buck—always the guardian, always attentive, and always near.

When you doubt His ending, and want to die . . . He says, "Write it now, while the pain is real," and fills the air with mock orange and sage; reminding you that you love to breathe.

When you rip out the *For Sale* signs . . . He says, "It takes more faith to leave them up."

When the weight of your secret is too much to bear . . . He sends the bobcat to be your "keeper of secrets." And each time you see him or walk in his tracks, you know your secret is safe.

When your feet are dragging in the dust . . . He says, "Lift your eyes," and with a golden eagle you learn to soar.

When you are impatient for lack of results . . . He leads you to the lake and walls, they are alive with unseen activity. Nests are being made, babies will be born; and only after much care, will they be ready to fly.

When you shout, "But what's the point?" . . . thunder rolls through the coulee, and wind ripples the lake like curled feathers. And as you watch you realize, this is the Place of Sage story—sometimes only slight as a feather, but in the end, the impact will be a wave.

And when your pain is too great . . . He says, "I am here, take My hand."

So when I asked, "But are you *sure* you want me to do this? . . . a rainbow sprung from the mesa, shot straight up, and arched over Place of Sage. At that point, I knew for sure, if I had done anything else, it would have been wrong.

Sometimes, something big comes along and takes our life by surprise . . . sound incredible? I know . . . and He is.

I've waited a long time to share this story with you. "Everything must be in place," He said. And finally, everything is.

Welcome to *Place of Sage*.

—Lyn Diane Nielsen

In our world of logic this makes no sense.
But, there are two worlds . . .
The first being greater than ours.
And in the first, the Master plans are made . . .
Place of Sage being one of them.

—Jamie Stemple
September 2, 1980

Chapter One

September 2, 2000

*R*iley, come on! We've got to hit the road."

Kayla Stemple donned jeans, boots, a man's white T-shirt—size small, and a ball cap to hold down wild blond hair. She grabbed her silver locket, loaded her arms with assorted duffle bags, and pushed through the front door of her little white house.

She should have expected it—today of all days—in lieu of their destination; but she didn't. Kayla cleared the last step when the words caught her by surprise— again.

"The time has come. You know what to do."

She spun around expecting to see someone, but of course she didn't. She never did. Only a voice in her right ear. A soft, masculine voice.

Why do I keep hearing this? I must be losing it.

She proceeded down the walk, tripped over a crack in the concrete, and launched herself into the white gate she was about to open. In a moment like this, some would curse and swear; Kayla shook her head. Lately it was happening a lot. She scrambled to her feet, looked around, and headed to her blue '68 Chevy Camaro, parked a few feet away.

The Saturday morning lawn ritual had begun. Like the domino effect of a yawn, it started with one mower, and soon the entire street buzzed; and young kids who escaped chores were out conquering the world, in the safety and confines of their own backyards.

"Hi, Kayla!" shouted two who broke free.

Kayla turned to see her blonde, blue-eyed neighbors pedaling their tricycles down the sidewalk.

"Hey, my favorite twins! Does your mom know you're out here?"

"Oh, she don't care—we're four now," said Jared.

"I think she—"

"Joseph and Jared Evans, you get back here this instant!" came from a nearby window.

"Uh-oh . . . bye, Kayla," Joseph said, while slowly waving.

She watched them turn their tricycles full circle and pedal at high speed up the sidewalk. She had to smile. They don't stay that size for long.

It was a great day to stay in Seattle. The scent of fresh-cut grass lingered in the air, music filtered out open windows, weathermen boasted a high of seventy-seven, and the whole city sparkled under the sun. Kayla wanted to celebrate with a walk to Green Lake and a good book, but today was not optional. There were bigger things planned for today. And in that place, down deep where the heart and mind connect, she knew it.

She fiddled with her key until the trunk sprung open; and in that same moment, her cell phone rang. The way she jumped, it could've been a snake. *What is wrong with me?* Kayla grabbed the culprit from the black bag, shoved it up to her ear, and knocked off her ball cap.

"Hello," she said, scooping up the hat.

"Hi, Honey! Have you left yet?"

"Dad . . . hi." Kayla leaned against the car. "No, I'm loading the trunk right now."

"Great! You'll be here early afternoon then."

"Yep," she said in her best attempt.

It was easy to picture her dad at the ranch: sitting at his desk, twirling his Aussie hat while he talked. Kayla smiled. Luke Stemple was still one of the most handsome men she knew—in a dark, rugged, outback kind of way.

"Kayla, are you okay? You sound like you slammed your finger in the door."

"No, I'm fine . . . just trying to get going."

She set her bags in the trunk, and pulled out the keys. Hearing his voice calmed down her insides. Just in time, too.

After slamming the front door, Riley Stemple stomped down the walk for all to see, and tossed her oversized gym bag in the trunk. Kayla smirked. If her green-eyed replica only knew how silly she looked.

"—I'm sorry, Dad—what'd you say?" Kayla stood still to listen.

"When you get here, I have something to give you . . . I've been saving it for the right time."

"Something for me? What is it?"

"It'll wait till you get here. Oh, and Kayla . . . don't forget my lima beans!"

The prospect of eating "dirt in little plastic skins" crinkled her nose. "I didn't forget."

She closed the trunk and headed for the driver's door; and Luke asked one last question.

"Kayla . . . what did you want to be when you grew up?"

She'd rather eat a lima bean. "Uh . . . Dad, I'm thirty-eight—I *am* grown up. It doesn't matter what I wanted to be." She kicked a piece of gravel near her tire. "I love you, Dad. We'll see you in a bit . . . bye." Kayla clicked off the phone, and slid in behind the wheel.

It was easy to ignore Riley's glare, she had her own thoughts eating at her. *Why did he ask me that after all these years . . . ? Accounting suits me—I like numbers. Oh brother . . . who am I kidding?*

After warming up the engine, they pulled up to the window of Starbucks. This was Seattle—espresso on every corner.

Kayla smiled her best at Riley. "What would you like? My treat."

Her grumbling eighteen-year-old leaned forward to read the menu. "An iced almond latte—double shot."

"Okay, and I'll have a regular coffee, with a touch of nonfat milk, please."

The young man acknowledged their order and disappeared.

Riley rolled her eyes. "It figures that you'd have plain old, boring coffee. Why don't you ever try something new?"

"Wow, Riley—thanks for the boost."

The exchange was made, and they were back in traffic.

Kayla tried a different tone. "Grandpa's excited to see you."

"Why?"

"Come on, Riley, you know how much this means to him."

Riley scrunched down in the seat, and flicked the thin pink straw in her drink. "Yeah, but does it have to be this weekend?"

"Of course it does—it's their anniversary!"

"Well, why can't he come here like he usually does?"

"Riley, don't start. I'm sorry you're missing Bumbershoot—and I realize it's Seattle's finest arts festival—but this is important, and Grandpa wants us at the ranch."

"Yeah . . . like you really want to go either, Mom. When was the last time *you* were there?"

Kayla let it slide, and tried to focus on juggling her boring coffee while merging onto Interstate 5. And since the freeway was always busy, she wasn't surprised when all four lanes halted in the downtown area.

But Riley wouldn't let it go. "Us having a party—that's insane."

Kayla shot her a look. Riley knew it well and stared up at the skyscrapers.

"Each new building is taller than the one before . . . when will it ever end?" She asked, not expecting her mom to answer.

Traffic moved again, and several horns behind them jolted Kayla back to the present. Riley slid down further as drivers pulled out around them. Strike two for Kayla.

It was a quiet drive from that point to Interstate 90—Seattle's link to rural Eastern Washington. But as they drove up the ramp, Riley blurted it out:

"This *is* insane—it's crazy—Grandma Jamie's dead!"

Chapter Two

*I*t took a mile for Kayla to compose herself.

"You're right. Grandma is gone. But Grandpa's not. And if he wants to celebrate their anniversary—that's exactly what we're going to do."

She couldn't continue. She needed to see the road, and wasn't prepared for tears. Neither was Riley.

"I'm sorry, Mom . . . I wish I could've met her."

Kayla fumbled with the radio, and after flipping through the entire FM selection, Riley asked:

"How old was she again?"

"She wasn't." Kayla cleared her throat. "She was only thirty-eight."

"Your age?"

Kayla nodded with a lump lodged in her voice box.

"And you were my age," Riley realized.

"Yep . . . ." Kayla whispered, and looked out her side window, drawing strength from sun-kissed water as they drove over Lake Washington.

"I can't imagine you not being here, Mom."

"I know."

A few miles later, Riley broke the silence. "Oh . . . and by the way, nice trip on the sidewalk this morning."

"Ugh, I was hoping you didn't see that. But thank you." Kayla bowed the best she could from the driver's seat. "Thank you very much!" The smile felt good to both of them.

"So, Mom . . . what did Grandpa Luke ask you on the phone?"

"I didn't know you were paying attention."

"I have very good ears. So why didn't you tell him you wanted to make films?"

"He knows—and how come you're so smart?"

"It doesn't take a genius to figure it out, Mom. You won't go on dates. You don't do anything with the girls from work—all you do for entertainment is rent movies and take notes. AND, you own a whole box of books on the subject."

"Not any more . . . we sold them at our last yard sale."

"Uh . . . well . . . *we* didn't. I couldn't let you do it, they're in my closet." Riley's eyes lit up. "I'll be happy to give them back to you."

"Donate them to the library—I won't use them . . . but thanks, Honey, that was sweet."

They came up fast behind a slow white minivan. Kayla made a hasty lane change and growled, "It's the pedal on the right."

Riley crossed her arms, and studied Kayla's face. "It's not too late, Mom. Look at me. I want to be an archaeologist, and we live in the middle of a city."

"Yeah . . . but you can do it. With your drive and stubborn Irish streak—you'll move mountains."

"I got that from Grandma Jamie, huh?"

"I guess so," Kayla mumbled.

Riley looked out her window, and sighed. "It doesn't matter anyways. I'll probably end up in a dumb job, just like you."

"Riley!"

"What? It's true."

"No it's not. And this 'dumb job' of mine has paid our bills, kept us in our home, and straightened *your* teeth."

"Yeah, but what about your dream, Mom? I know you got as far as film school, because that's where you met Dad. What I don't get, is why you gave it all up."

"You're just full of questions, aren't you?"

"Yep, and I'm just warming up." Riley stretched her arms for effect.

"Great." Kayla leaned on her elbow. "We've been over this before. I couldn't support us, and go to film school at the same time—we were broke when your dad left."

"But how could he do that? How does a person just walk away?"

"I don't know, Riley—what is it with minivans to-day?" Kayla swerved around another one. "—A family didn't fit his career plans. When we got married, he was almost done with school; but I was just getting started. And then, when he found out we were going to be parents, well . . . let's just drop it, okay?"

Riley wasn't as ready for that as she thought she was. And when she slumped down even more, Kayla grabbed her arm.

"Hey, we're doing all right." She wiggled Riley's arm until a smile broke through.

"Mom, do you think we'll see him again some-day?"

"I don't know . . . maybe in film credits. He was good."

Riley sat up straight. "Yeah, well you're better."

"Okay new topic," Kayla said, and looked at the view like a child waking from a nap. "It's amazing how fast we go from concrete and steel, to the foothills dressed in evergreens."

"How poetic, Mom . . . and you say you're not a storyteller." Riley looked out the window and perked up. "All right—new topic. Let's talk about Grandma Jamie's book."

Kayla noticed a quick diversion. "Let's talk about boys instead."

Riley raised her eyebrows. *"Why?"*

"There's a carload next to us, and they're all gawk-ing at you."

Riley glanced over at the souped-up Mustang, and turned back to Kayla. "Now then, where were we?"

Ugh, that was short. Kayla scrolled through ideas, and thought she had a winner. "Hey, let's stop at Snoqualmie Falls. I hear it's beautiful this time of year."

Riley nodded. "That's great . . . as long as we can talk about the book. Did you know I've read it four times?"

Kayla squirmed. "I knew I hadn't seen it for a while."

"It's with me . . . and I've been thinking about it a lot."

An alarm went off in Kayla's head, and she held her breath for Riley's next line, knowing full well what was coming.

"Grandma Jamie called it fiction . . . but it's real, isn't it?"

Kayla froze looking straight ahead.

"Why don't you talk about it, Mom? It's an incredible book. And if this story's true, and part of my roots, then I need to hear it—all of it—the whole story of *Place of Sage*—and you need to tell it!"

"Is that so?" Kayla mustered through a tight jaw.

"Yes!" Riley sat up tall. "Okay . . . now in the story, God tells Teri it's time to make this major move—but in real life, if Teri is Grandma Jamie, then how did she know it was time to move?"

Kayla wasn't up for this. "Well, think about it, Riley. If the book is a true story—then what does that tell you?"

Riley sat up even straighter. "So God *did* talk to Grandma Jamie? And all those things she wrote about—really *did* happen?"

"That's what she claimed."

"Well, what do you think, Mom?"

Kayla fidgeted a bit. "I don't know yet."

"*YET?* You've had twenty years to think about it!"

"Riley!"

"What?"

Riley crossed her arms and stared at Kayla. "Well if Grandma Jamie wrote it, then I believe her . . . but it must have been hard."

"It was . . . on everyone."

"Keep talking, Mom—I need to know everything."

"Riley, I don't think this is the time—"

"Sure it is. We're stuck in this car for nearly four hours—what else are we gonna do? Pleeease. Start at the beginning, and I'll try not to interrupt."

"I—I can't just start talking about it—I need to think about it . . . organize my thoughts."

Riley looked out her side window; then smiled at Kayla. "Mom . . . when has that ever stopped you? You can tell a story better than anyone I know. Come on, pleeease?"

Kayla made the mistake of looking at her daughter. It worked every time: the pouting puppy face, complete with quivering lower lip.

"I'll think about it—okay?"

"Great! Take the whole five minutes if you need to."

Kayla shook her head. But it was true. Riley didn't know much about her roots. Kayla told herself she was waiting until Riley was old enough to understand. But the truth was, it was easier to avoid the subject—she didn't understand it either. And in the meantime, her years with Riley had slipped by.

Kayla softened, as every nerve ending in her body objected. "Okay, but just the trip over—and we listen to music of my choice on the drive home."

"Deal."

Riley was patient as Kayla's mind swirled with activity: a piece of this year, a swatch from that; and soon, the emotion she had packed up at eighteen, moved back in.

Kayla watched for her escape as they came around the bend. "Cool—there's our exit," she said. *Saved by the falls*, she thought.

"Okay, but this doesn't get you off the hook," Riley said, in a tone too much like a parent.

"Of course not." *But one can hope.*

"I brought my camera along," Riley added, "so let's shoot a few pictures."

"Uh-huh," Kayla mumbled.

They pulled into the park entrance and surveyed the busy area. Parents and kids—knee-high to teens, were spending time together before the school year began. Since Riley was going away to college, their summer would last a few more weeks. Kayla was grateful for that.

They joined other families en route to the lookout. It was a small walk around Douglas fir trees, picnic tables and benches. The stretch felt good, and the view was even better.

Snoqualmie Falls roared as it fell 268 feet to the wooded gorge below; creating a spray that rose back to the top like steam. Kayla leaned on the rail and breathed in the thick forest air. She understood why Indians sought out the falls as a place of peace. The sound alone helped her to relax.

After pictures, they followed a walkway of Flowering cherry and maple leaves that led to the well-known Salish Lodge and Spa. Built at the crest of the falls, it sat like a brown castle on top of the rock crag. Riley was quick to recognize it as she snapped a picture.

"Hey, Mom. Isn't this where that show was filmed—ohhh, what was the name of it?"

"Twin Peaks" Kayla replied, rather quickly.

"Yeah . . . that's the one. That was a strange show . . . ."

A wedding was taking place on a small covered deck, and they stopped a moment to watch. Riley commented on the dresses while Kayla thought of Jamie and Luke.

"—Don't you? Mom . . . ? You didn't hear a word I said, did you?"

"I'm sorry—what?"

"The wedding colors—I think black and white looks great, don't you?"

"Uh . . . yeah, it looks good," Kayla whispered.

"Where were you just now?"

Kayla bit at her lip. "Grandma and Grandpa had the same colors at their wedding."

There was a long pause. An older couple passed by, and a breeze rustled leaves around them.

"They really loved each other, huh, Mom?"

"Yeah . . . they really did." Kayla leaned in against the rail, and continued—much to her own surprise.

"Here were two people, who knew at a very young age they were meant to be together . . . so they waited for each other to grow up." Tears she didn't expect slipped out. "My heart still hurts at the thought of one without the other."

Riley put her arm through Kayla's, and they proceeded along the path.

"Mom, do you think you'll ever get married again?"

Kayla almost tripped as they approached the car.

"Uh . . . I don't know . . . I'm not planning on it."

"Well if you were, what would he be like?"

"I don't know . . . opposite of the first one I guess. And a whole lot like your grandpa." She paused, and then added, "right down to the Australian Outback hat, and long oilskin coat."

"Oh! Like *The Man from Snowy River*."

"I suppose so."

"Good luck finding him in the middle of Seattle," Riley said with a smirk.

"Very funny, Riley, I'm not looking."

"Well, maybe you should. I'm not gonna be at home much longer."

Kayla had no comment; it was easier that way. But the thought grabbed her heart and twisted it clockwise.

Back on the road, Riley was prompt as church bells. "Okay, Mom, start talking; I want the whole story."

Ready or not—and she wasn't—the time had come.

Kayla struggled with a starting point. And then like a barn full of wet hay, internal combustion resulted and she blurted out:

"Riley, this story—that book . . . it almost destroyed our family." She stopped a moment before continuing. "For eleven years, using up his weekends, Grandpa worked to restore our Victorian home in Seattle. It was beautiful . . . every room trimmed in wood. Then all of a sudden, we were plucked away, and plunked in a one-bedroom house—in a speck of a town—in the middle of a wheat field!"

Riley frowned. "I take it you weren't thrilled with the move?"

"No! It didn't make sense that we would move nearly three hundred miles away—and leave your grandpa Luke behind."

Kayla hesitated; then continued. "But, there was a lot that didn't make sense . . . a lot of things none of us knew at the time . . . ."

Riley piped up. "Well, what about Uncle Chris? What'd he think?"

"He was glad, at first; the city was taking a toll on him. It was the seventies: too many ways for a kid to get high."

The sign read: "Snoqualmie Pass - 19 miles." And for the most part, all nineteen were driven in silence, on a worn, cracked freeway that weaved up through the tall forest of the Cascade Mountains. Kayla knew that for Riley to be so quiet, she had to be analyzing what had been said, and undoubtedly making comparisons to Jamie's book.

They reached the summit at an ear popping 3,022 feet. A woman watered flowers on the deck of a small

A-frame; and above her, the ski lifts sat empty and out of place against the green mountainside. At the very top, the peak was blocked by fog, much the same way Kayla's brain was blocked from forming logical, complete thoughts on Jamie's story.

The descent reminded her of a go-cart race, not that Kayla would know about such things, she was never in a go-cart race; but at that particular moment, she pondered just about anything to avoid the subject at hand . . .

The ruts in the road have a sign in their honor—maybe someone's idea of cheap road maintenance.

The trees aren't so tall next to the freeway. Oh! They're only the top halves.

You certainly can't see the forest through the trees.

The fall colors are like a box of crayons . . . and just how many shades of green are there?

"Come on, Mom! I've been waiting over an hour for this story. If you need incentive—just think of Rap music and my driving for the trip home."

That helped to pull Kayla back. And it was true. They were now in the land of Ponderosa pines; which meant Riley had been patient for nearly seventy-five miles. The temperature had jumped a few degrees, and as Kayla rolled down her window, the rich scent of pine helped her memory along.

"Okay," Riley said, holding up her hand, "A new deal. You tell me the story—the whole story—from the beginning; and I'll buy coffee on the trip home, *and* let you listen to that country stuff you like." She saw

Kayla's frown, and added, "Just tell it like a movie, Mom. You're good at that."

If asked, Kayla could not have described the miles between Riley's suggestion and the turn off for Roslyn. But Riley knew exactly where they were, and piped up again.

"Okay, we'll start with a small detour through Roslyn—for inspiration. That *is* where *Northern Exposure* was filmed, right?

Kayla couldn't help but smile, and nodded in agreement as she prepared to exit the freeway.

The beauty of a forest in Eastern Washington is that you *can* see the forest through the trees.

As they drove off the interstate, and turned left at the stop sign, they both spotted the same tree. It wasn't a pine, and they weren't sure what it was. Half way up the tree, the trunk split into two trunks, one dead and one alive. The dead part had gray, scraggly branches that were bent and gnarled, and the live part had white branches and green leaves that worked hard to get around the dead part.

Kayla's first thought about the tree was that it mirrored her life perfectly. It was okay to think it, but she wasn't thrilled when her perceptive daughter verbalized it.

"You're kind of like that tree . . . aren't you, Mom?"

Kayla heard herself reply, "I guess I am."

At that moment of realization, something brewed below the surface. On one hand, Kayla wanted to scream; but on the other, something else was going on—an excitement she couldn't explain, coming from a place she didn't understand.

They drove the two-lane road into Roslyn, and it was easy to picture this town in snow. A gas station shared space with a snowmobile dealer; and colorful, steep-pitched, metal roofs topped the homes.

At the main intersection, they turned left onto Pennsylvania Avenue, and Riley practically leaped in the back seat for the camera.

"Mom, go there! I want a picture of the Roslyn Cafe mural."

Kayla enjoyed her enthusiasm, and drove down the block. The best shot was from the street they were on, and when Riley yelled, "stop!" Kayla did, much to the frustration of the guy behind them. By the way he shook his head, he must have been a local. Kayla wondered what he thought of Roslyn's fame since the popular television series.

As Riley stood in the middle of the street for that perfect shot, Kayla saw her resemblance to Jamie. But, before she could grasp a specific instance, Riley was back in the car, beaming.

"Cool!" Riley said. "I love that mural: snow-capped mountains and a forest—sharing space with sand, a camel standing in water, and palm trees. It's great! The only thing missing is the moose."

"Huh? Oh, yeah . . . *Northern Exposure* . . . ."

"We'll have to watch that show, Mom—it's still on, isn't it?"

"I think so . . . on A&E, we'll have to check."

And the brewing continued.

She turned the car around, drove to the coal miner's memorial, and turned right on the road leading out of town. Her thoughts drifted back to that tree. She thought about how well it would do if the dry trunk and branches were cut away, allowing the live side to grow straight and tall, instead of trying to grow around the dead part.

As they approached the interstate, Kayla watched for the tree. As they drove by it, she heard the voice again, softly in her right ear.

"The time has come. The story is yours."

She quickly turned to Riley, hoping for a reaction.

"What?" Riley asked, wondering what the strange look was for.

"Nothing." Kayla shook her head. *Now I know I'm losing it.*

But . . . for the first time in her life, for reasons she didn't understand, she had a sense of why Jamie did what she did.

She couldn't explain it. Butterflies the size of birds danced in her stomach, and in that place, down deep, she knew . . . she would stay like that tree, if she didn't tell Jamie's story.

She waited a moment, hoping the symptoms would leave. They didn't. She looked over at Riley, and a current of energy ran through her spine.

"So . . . you want a movie, huh?" She asked feeling heat from head to toe. "Okay." And like a person taking a giant leap, she took a deep breath—

"Fade in."

Chapter Three

August 27, 1976

Jamie, Kayla, and Chris stood on the crooked front porch of the little white house. The mosquitoes were thick, and hungry; but the neighbors didn't seem to mind as they stood outside to stare.

Luke came out with coffee as hot as the evening. He hugged Kayla, the spitting image of Jamie; and Chris, who at fourteen, had his same broad shoulders, dark hair and blue eyes. Then he turned to Jamie.

"I'll see you next weekend."

Jamie hugged him tight, and he whispered in her ear. "I'm trusting you, James. Don't forget your promise."

He smiled at his kids, and got back in the U-haul truck he drove over just hours before. With a backdrop of grain elevators and a sunset, Adalon's new residents waved until he was out of sight.

"*What?* Do we look like aliens or something?" Chris shouted to the neighbors watching them.

"Chris!" Jamie pulled him in the house. "It's a small town . . . we're probably today's main attraction."

"Well, I don't like to be stared at," he said, eyeing the boxes. "Have you seen my Led Zeppelin album?"

"It's here somewhere. Check the boxes in your room."

"Great," he grumbled, and walked to his makeshift bedroom in the laundry room.

"This is strange," Kayla said, and headed towards the one real bedroom.

Alone in the front room—which would have to serve as living room, dining room, office, and her bedroom—Jamie walked in a circle before sitting amongst the boxes.

"What have I done?" she whispered.

Her moment of doubt was interrupted by the lyrics of "Stairway to Heaven," which was naturally followed by Kayla yelling from the bedroom door.

"Mom, make him turn it down. I can't hear myself think."

Jamie chuckled—that was her line. She got up from the floor, walked through the small kitchen, and knocked on Chris' door.

"All right, All right," was heard through the door, as the last line of the song grew dim. Jamie knocked on the door again, and this time it opened.

"Thanks, Chris. It's a small house—it's going to take some getting used to."

"No kidding," Chris said, pulling Jethro Tull and The Moody Blues from a box marked "Chris' records—Fragile!"

"And tell Kayla this is my room. Just because the washer and dryer are in here—that doesn't mean she can barge in whenever she wants."

"Don't worry, she knows. And I'm proud of you—you're being a good sport about this. Just remember . . . it's only for a little while."

"Are you sure?"

"Oh yeah, it'll be great. You'll see."

"I hope so," Chris said, moving his record player for the third time. "But couldn't we've bought a bigger house?"

Jamie rubbed his shoulder, and walked back to the front room. It was late, and unlike Seattle, the temperature didn't go down as soon as the sun did. At eleven o'clock it was still eighty-nine degrees.

Jamie stepped out on the porch, hoping for stars and a breeze. What she got instead was a cricket choir, and an illuminated cross on the church down the street—it had to be twelve feet high to be so visible.

"Father, please keep Luke safe for me," she whispered, "and help him to understand." She stared at the cross a moment longer. "And thank you for getting us here."

In the stillness of this new land, she knew she was not alone—exhausted, nervous, and missing Luke already—but not alone. She breathed in the warm, dry air, and went inside. When she spied the soft black cover of her journal, it was like finding an old friend.

She cleared off the brown tweed sofa, curled up on one end, and began to write.

August 27, 1976:

So how do I feel about being here? Like someone who woke from a dream, and then wondered if it was real. I can't believe we made it this far, with all the problems it took to get here.

It's so crazy to think I based this decision on a voice; but that's exactly what I did. The One who said, "This is the way, walk in it."

In my heart I feel the place we're headed to. We just haven't seen it yet. But I know we will.

Jamie put the book and pen on her lap, leaned into the sofa and closed her eyes.

At daybreak, farm machinery rumbled down Main Street. Jamie jumped up and struggled with clattering metal blinds to catch a glimpse.

So this is rush hour.

She chuckled, pulled her blonde hair in a knot, and headed for the coffee pot. She knew exactly what box to look in, and within minutes, the aroma of strong brew filled the tiny kitchen. She preferred coffee with a touch of milk, but the old Kelvinator refrigerator didn't come stocked; so this morning it was black or none. She chose black, and surveyed the room.

Wallpaper covered the walls—a jungle theme of lime green leaves on a white background. Next, Jamie checked the cupboards like a guest in a hotel; they were all in good shape, except for being lime green.

With coffee in hand, she headed through the dining area—actually a thoroughfare between bedroom, bath and kitchen—to get to the living room.

Someone had a fondness for this green; it was in every room. Even the living room wore green plaid on the walls and green carpeting on the floor. At least the ceiling was white.

Jamie looked at the stacked boxes surrounding her, and suddenly felt sick. *What if I was wrong about this?* After a moment of struggle, she exhaled and went in search of a towel. Her head ached, but she chalked that up to the climate change, and knew a shower would help.

And it did. By the time Jamie was dressed in a tank top and shorts, she was raring to go. She came around the kitchen corner, and ran into Kayla who was rubbing her eyes like a small child.

"Good morning, Punkin!"

"Mom, I'm fifteen. Do you have to call me 'Punkin'?"

"Yes I do," Jamie said, as she poured more coffee and grabbed a cinnamon bagel.

Kayla looked around and shook her head. "Where's our table gonna go? There's no room for it."

Jamie pointed to the dining area. "It'll fit. We'll push it up against the wall, and use two chairs on the ends."

"But there's four of us."

"It'll work for now," Jamie said, biting into the bagel.

Kayla nodded her infamous "yeah, right" nod, and went back in the bedroom. Jamie took two aspirin and knuckled down to unpacking.

Soon both kids were organizing their own space, in their own way. Kayla folded her clothes and put them in proper drawer order. Chris used a special method: open a drawer and tip a box.

At noon, the chimes on the church belted out "Amazing Grace," and the trio raced to the door to see what was happening. No cars. No people. Only music that intensified with the breeze.

"This is different," Chris said, as he and Kayla both shrugged.

On that note, they left to explore the town and grab a few things at the store. Jamie went back to unpacking.

But, within the hour, the two drug themselves back in the house, moaning about the heat. "It must be a hundred degrees out there," Chris whined, pulling Sunny Delight from the brown grocery bag, "and I'm starving!"

"It's a hundred and one," Kayla said. "Let's make lunch."

"So, Mom," Chris called from the kitchen, "did you know you moved us to a place with rattlesnakes? Big ones! Just last week someone found one that was five feet long. Now don't you feel safe?" Chris stared at Kayla, with animated eyebrows.

Without looking up Jamie answered, "Cool, now use a glass, please."

He expected a better reaction. Jamie smiled and said, "You guys weren't gone long, did you see the whole town?"

Kayla was quick to respond. "Town? Mom, I've heard of small towns, but this is ridiculous. This town is so small I can name everything on two hands." She held up her hands to demonstrate. "A grocery store, post office, one bank—the one being built doesn't count, besides it blew down in the wind storm; two taverns, two churches, an implement store—whatever that is, a hardware store, half a library, and City hall. Ten and a half."

"And two gas stations," Chris added.

"Okay—twelve and a half."

"Thirteen and a half. You forgot the newspaper office," Jamie announced.

Chris and Kayla rolled their eyes, and continued making lunch.

"Well, talk about small," Chris said, "I heard there's only gonna be twenty-six kids in the eighth grade. That's hardly enough to find a friend."

"There's always your pet rock," Kayla smirked.

"Ha, ha—real funny."

After ten minutes of bantering, they had three plates ready with grilled cheese sandwiches, Bugles, and the largest pickles in the jar.

By sunset, everything that would fit had been unpacked, and the rest was by the sliding door, in the dining area, waiting to join chairs in the garage. Jamie didn't complain—how could she? Yes, the house was barely nine hundred square feet, and yes, she hated lime green, but it got them here—at a time when there was nothing for sale.

Before falling asleep, Jamie opened the blinds enough to see the illuminated cross from the sofa. "Father, please watch over Luke, and keep him safe," she whispered.

At two in the morning, she sat straight up, and tried to orient herself. She looked around the semi-dark room, and tried to recall where she had just been. Then she turned on the lamp, scrambled for her journal and pen, and wrote as fast as she could.

August 29, 1976:

How I got there, and where I was, I don't know. But it was too splendid to be real.

The sunset splashed a rose hue across tall basalt walls, and the rock slopes and canyon floor were colored with new grass, fresh sage, and dots of purple and white lupine.

I wanted to stay forever. I felt peace, such as never before.

In the distance, I heard a wind rushing through the coulee. It moved closer, like a wave about to crash on shore. But it didn't. Instead of a crescendo, it swooped me up in one gentle gust, up to where a golden eagle soared.

He blinked at me, and together we soared between rock walls—as if this were an everyday happening. I could hear the wind, it rushed all around me; but not a single strand of my hair moved. We circled over a small, heart-shaped lake—with water as blue as Luke's eyes; and then landed on a mesa standing alone in the coulee. I could still hear the wind, but all I felt was calm.

The eagle blinked, rose up in the air, and disappeared. The wind ceased, meadowlarks sang, and the air was filled with sage perfume.

At five-forty, farm machinery rumbled down Main Street. *Who needs a rooster?* Jamie thought, and stumbled to the kitchen. She didn't know much about farming; but she was trying. So far, she knew that the winter wheat harvest was finishing up, and a rush was on to get seed wheat in the ground for next year's crop.

As her coffee brewed, the aroma filled the kitchen; but Jamie inhaled sage. She grabbed her journal and read the last entry. *What does it mean?* She dropped bread in the toaster, poured coffee, and continued to stare at the page. *It couldn't be. Could it?* But then logic set in. She tucked the journal in her box of writing books and flute music, and got on with the day.

After a shower, Jamie threw on jeans with no knees, a man's small white T-shirt, and an old pair of tennis shoes. She plunked on a ball cap, tucked the silver locket in her shirt, and headed out the sliding door. With tons of work to do, she was glad to start early—like the farmers and the birds.

Flowers and grass that wrapped the house were beyond dry. Even weeds crunched under foot. From the garage, Jamie grabbed a rake, shovel, and a rusty old pail discarded in the corner. She turned to exit the dim, dusty catchall, and was cornered by a frantic Kayla.

"Mom, I can't find my wedge sandals and blue halter top!"

"Did you check all your boxes?"

"Yes—and I need them for tomorrow!"

"*Tomorrow?* You're not wearing a halter top to school. No way."

Kayla stomped back in the house. Jamie shook her head, walked to the front yard, and was ambushed by a petite lady with short silver hair, a bright smile, and a loaf of homemade bread.

"Hello! I'm Milly Edwards."

"Hi . . . Jamie Stemple."

"I know, welcome to Adalon!"

Jamie put down her tools as Milly held out the loaf wrapped in cellophane and a red ribbon. "Fresh from the oven!"

That's really nice of you," Jamie said, accepting the warm gift. "Thank you."

Milly went right to the nuts-and-bolts. "So . . . rumor has it you're a writer with teenage kids. Are you married?"

"Married, yes, and I do have two great kids."

"And you're a writer?"

"Um . . . well . . . I'm working on it."

Milly's eye twinkled as she asked, "Do you write everyday?"

"Yes."

"Then you're a writer."

Jamie held the bread close to her nose. "This smells great. I haven't had homemade bread for years. Mom tried to teach me, but her talent didn't rub off."

Milly's eyes twinkled again. "Well, if you think about it, making bread is a lot like writing a story."

Jamie's nose crinkled, and Milly continued.

"First you add all the ingredients—right? Then you mix it up, let it rest, and work it again. Then, when it's your best work; it moves on—to a publisher, or in my case, the oven—for its final form. And then the best part: after the labor comes the reward.

"That's pretty good . . . maybe you should be the writer."

"Nope—that's your calling. But, if you get a hankering for a good potato bread, come on over—I'm only two streets that way, in the yellow house." She pointed to the left, and asked her next question. "You're from the coast, right?"

"No, Seattle. Puget Sound touches Seattle; but the ocean is still a hundred and thirty-some miles west."

"Well, get used to it. Around here, if you come from the west side of the mountains—you come from the coast."

"Hmm, what a concept."

"So why here, Jamie? How does a writer from Seattle end up in Adalon?"

Jamie shuffled her weight from one foot to another, and considered the gravity of the question.

"It's a long story."

From inside the house came, "Shut up, Chris!" followed by, "Shut up, yourself—you're not the boss of me!"

A door slammed shut, causing old windows to rattle in loose frames. Jamie and Milly waited; and on cue, the second door followed, with music that was audible two blocks away.

"Well . . . those would be my 'two great kids.'"

Milly giggled. "I better run. You're busy; and I promised a letter to my sister in Kansas. But, Jamie, I love a good story . . . and I'm looking forward to yours."

"Well, thank you again for the bread."

Milly squeezed her hand. "God bless you, Jamie . . . I hope to see you soon."

Jamie watched her hurry out the front gate, and had a strange feeling she knew more than she let on.

Another door slammed, and Jamie went inside to defuse the situation. She knocked on Chris' door, and waited for him to turn down the music.

"What's going on, Chris?"

"Nothing, Mom."

"Oh." She paused a moment. "Okay." She paused another moment. "Well . . . I'll be out here if you need me." She paused at Kayla's door, then went back outside and pulled up the sad remains of what used to be yellow iris.

A few minutes later, Chris appeared at the sliding door in Levi cut-offs, a T-shirt, and his basketball twirling on one finger.

"Why does school start so early here? It's too hot to be in school."

Jamie didn't answer, knowing there was more.

"I don't want to go to school in this stupid town— they're all dorks. And they wear Wrangler jeans—I don't belong here."

He let the ball fall on a cracked concrete step, and kicked it towards the front gate. "I'm gonna look for a hoop."

Jamie watched him bounce the basketball down the street. *He'll find his way.*

In short order, Kayla stomped out and threw a newspaper on the porch.

"How am I suppose to keep up with films when the closest theatre is an hour away—and they don't even show current pictures."

Jamie looked up. "What?"

"*The Hindenburg.* I saw it in Seattle two weeks ago—and it's just now playing over here. This is ridiculous!"

Jamie smiled. *My future filmmaker.*

After a sleepless night, it was time to face the first day of school. Alarms went off early, and it was a fight to see whose music was the loudest, and who had first dibs on the bathroom. After a brief skirmish, Kayla hopped in the shower; Chris cranked up Pink Floyd's "Dark Side of the Moon"; and Jamie was in the kitchen, drinking coffee and putting out breakfast options. But unfortunately, she didn't drink enough, soon enough, to be ready for what happened next . . . .

Chris burst from his room pointing out red bumps on his face and chest; Kayla came around the corner screaming, "I can't be seen like this!" and Jamie opened a cupboard that startled a mouse, that flew off the Raisin Bran, bounced off her shoulder, and hit the floor running. She dropped her coffee, and the three stared at each other, wearing the same expression and the same red bumps.

Kayla shouted, "We have chicken pox! Our first day at a new school—and we have chicken pox."

Jamie cleaned up the coffee, and took a deep breath. "Okay, let's calm down. We don't have the chicken pox—we've all had them before. What we *do* have is a bad case of mosquito bites, and one scared mouse."

"I don't know, Mom, remember Debbie Schultz? She had them when we were in first grade, and got them again in eighth grade. And even if it's not—look at my face!"

"Kayla, your face is fine, and I think Mom's right. It's the mosquitoes—they're really bad over here."

"Try not to scratch them," Jamie called out, as she rummaged through a drawer in the bathroom. "I have some lotion that will help—but you guys have got to get ready for school. You'll be fine."

Both kids shook their heads.

"Great," Kayla mumbled, pushing Chris through his room to get to the dryer.

"Kayla, did you see that mouse fly out at Mom?"

"And did you see the look on her face?"

Chris re-enacted the event, and they burst out laughing.

Jamie leaned against the sink. *And this is only day three.*

"Wait a minute! Cut." Riley held up her hands.

Kayla noticed the landscape. The pines, for the most part, had given way to sage. They were three miles from Kittitas, and almost half way there.

"What was the promise?" Riley asked. "I don't remember any promise in the book."

"It was there," Kayla said, still studying the familiar terrain, ". . . before they moved . . . Teri promised Paul she'd get a normal job, so he could move over."

"So Grandma Jamie made the same promise to Grandpa Luke?"

Kayla nodded.

"You mean, Grandpa Luke didn't believe in her writing? But she wrote a best-selling novel."

Kayla shifted about for a moment, and kept her eyes on the road. "That's not a fair statement, Riley—back then she hadn't sold anything. She needed to get a paying job as much as Teri did."

"So she did right?"

"Who—Teri?"

"No—Grandma Jamie. I know what Teri did."

"Well . . . her intentions were true, just like Teri's. But days flipped into months; Grandma wouldn't stop writing, and as the weather worsened so did their situation. And with your Grandpa trying to get home on the weekends, well . . . what could have been a winter wonderland, wasn't so wonderful."

Chapter Four

"I'M KING OF THE MOUNTAIN!" Chris shouted, with arms lifted high.

Then, in a quick plot to shorten his reign, disloyal subjects commenced an attack from all sides of the ten-foot snow fortress.

Jamie turned onto Main Street in time to view the treasonous act. As she drove by what used to be the bank parking lot (but now a handy spot to pile snow), the warriors waved, and continued to dethrone her son with snowballs. She had to smile. For a boy who didn't want to be here, he'd become quite popular.

A dump truck zoomed by with a load of snow, and Jamie wondered where they were taking it. It had to go somewhere. And according to the forecast, it wasn't going to melt any time soon. But Adalon looked good in white, and so different than any other time of year.

Main Street had acquired a lane divider—just like main arterials in Seattle. The only difference was, this one stayed as long as the mercury was below thirty-two. It was a clever use for snow, as long as you didn't need to make a left turn.

Further down the street, in the middle of the street, six community-minded men were putting up the annual Adalon Christmas tree. And with a little help from a John Deere tractor, the tall Douglas fir rose gracefully into place. The tree was beautiful, yes, but to Jamie it was a reminder that four months had passed; she had no income, and no specific direction.

She parked in front of her little white house, slumped down in the seat, and closed her eyes to keep tears and a headache at bay. *Father, please show me what to do.*

Seconds later, a snowball smacked the windshield. Jamie jumped, and Kayla dashed out from behind the big pine tree.

"Mom, good news—I got a job! It's only a dollar-ninety an hour, but at least it's something."

Jamie managed a smile. "Congratulations. I'm proud of you. Now you'll be able to get some of the things you've wanted . . . and have been sweet enough not to ask for."

"Yeah, like some new clothes—and movie tickets. I can't wait to see a film again!"

A week later, there were two storms in Adalon. One added six inches of snow to a frozen twelve-inch base;

high winds for drifts; and a whiteout that shut down the mountain pass. But the other was worse.

Chris, Kayla, and enough snow to fill a salad bowl, blew in through the front door.

Kayla punched her brother. "Shhhh, Mom's on the phone."

Jamie didn't look up.

"I'm sorry, Luke," she said, and rubbed tears from her chin. ". . . We'll just wait till the pass reopens, then we'll have Christmas together."

There was no answer on Luke's end.

"I love you, Luke . . . ."

Jamie handed the phone to Chris, walked in the bathroom, and locked both doors. She took two more aspirin, and leaned against the wall.

"What have I done?" she whispered.

"Mom, are you all right?" Kayla turned the door-knob, and put her ear against the door. "Mom?"

Jamie rubbed the back of her head, and pulled herself away from the wall. "I'm fine. I'll be out in a few minutes."

"Okay, but wait till you see what's in the living room."

Jamie splashed her face with cold water, and took a deep breath when she looked in the mirror. She wasn't fine—and she knew it.

Chris pounded on the door. "Mom, come out here."

Jamie opened the door, and Chris pulled her through the bedroom and out to the living room.

"We don't know who it's from. There was a knock on the door, and when we opened it, this fell in."

Jamie took one look at the Christmas tree standing in the corner, and burst into tears. Kayla and Chris looked at each other, not sure if they should laugh.

Chris patted the top of Jamie's head. "It's okay, Mom . . . it's just a tree."

Chapter Five

"Dad, before you go, what's your New Year's resolution?" Kayla asked.

Luke stopped walking towards the door, and looked at Jamie. "To never do this again."

Chris pulled him in for a bear hug. "I wish you didn't have to leave so soon, Dad, you just got here."

"Sorry, guys, but if I don't leave now, I'll be driving in the dark on a sheet of ice."

The kids stood on the crooked porch, while Jamie walked Luke to his white '72 Chevy truck. The preheated engine hummed, and warm air escaped the cab when he threw in his duffle bag. Jamie folded down the collar of his lined jacket, and held him tight.

"Don't forget your promise, James . . . please."

"I haven't," she said, as Luke pulled away and got in the truck.

Once again, the three waved until he was out of sight.

Father, please keep Luke safe for me.

"Mom, why does Dad call you James?" Kayla asked. "That's not a girl's name."

"It is when your dad says it." Jamie said, trying to be cheerful.

Kayla and Chris shrugged their shoulders. "Okay, well I guess the holiday's over," Kayla stated. "Do you want us to take down the tree?"

"Might as well."

Jamie took laundry detail, while Kayla and Chris packed up the decorations.

"I wish we'd stayed in Seattle," Chris said, abruptly.

Kayla shook her head. "No you don't. We're doing better here."

"Oh—yeah. Look at us. Dad can't live with us; we have no privacy, no money—yeah—you're right—it's much better here." He threw a gold ornament in the box.

Kayla picked it up and checked for cracks. "Dad will move over—as soon as they can afford it. And at least we have a room—think of Dad and Mom. He lives in a job shack at work, and she sleeps on that lumpy couch. And its not like we're starving."

Chris lowered his voice. "Yeah, but it would help if Mom got a job."

"I know," Kayla whispered.

They didn't realize Jamie heard every word.

It was colder the next morning. Even the neighborhood dogs stayed in. Jamie hurried down the walk to warm up her burgundy '73 Buick Century. She tried hard not to inhale—it was like sucking up ice crystals. She shouldn't have touched the door handle with a bare hand, but she did; and to prolong the pain, it wouldn't open.

"Come on!" she said, as arctic wind cut through her wool suit like it wasn't even there.

Finally, the door opened. She jumped in and turned the key. Nothing. She turned the key again. Nothing. Not even lights.

"Not today . . . please . . . ."

A boy scout she wasn't; but Jamie *was* prepared for a few things. She pulled a crescent wrench from under the seat, and jumped out to open the hood. She tapped on the battery connectors, and wiggled the cables. She even popped open the cell caps, hoping for a quick cure. After a few minutes, her fingers were red, throbbing, and slow to bend. She stepped back and kicked the tire.

"You stupid car!"

"Mom, what's wrong?" Kayla called from the front door.

Jamie shouted back. "It won't start—How am I suppose to go job hunting if the stupid car won't start? I hate this car!"

"Uh . . . ."

Kayla ran to the bedroom, grabbed two pairs of gloves, and ran out the front door.

"Mom, you shouldn't be out here with your hands exposed—haven't you heard of frostbite?"

"I haven't been out that long."

"It doesn't take as long as you think—and trust me, you don't want to get it. We studied it in health. And why aren't you wearing your long coat?"

"Because I didn't plan to be out this long—and who's the parent here anyways? Now give me a hand, go try to start it." Jamie felt her right hand. The skin on her fingers was cold, numb, hard and pale.

Kayla hurried to the driver's seat. Jamie heard the key click over, but nothing more. Kayla made several more attempts.

"All right, Kayla, thank you."

"I'm sorry, Mom."

"Yeah . . . me too." Jamie slammed down the hood.

"Well, you always tell me there's a reason for everything. Maybe you're supposed to stay home today . . . maybe, do a little writing? You're going to be a great writer someday, Mom."

"Thanks, Kayla, but don't you have a bus to catch?"

"Nope. I've got a ride this morning."

They shivered their way in the house, and Jamie went straight to the kitchen sink for warm water. A few minutes later, the kids left for school and the house was still. The soak didn't seem to help her right hand, and the fingers felt like they were being stabbed with invisible knives. She took Kayla's advice and tucked them in a soft white glove.

Jamie wandered around as the pain intensified. Her thumb, index, and middle finger were blotched with dark red—nearly black—patches; and when she eased off the glove, they burned from exposure to air.

At four o'clock, Jamie was still walking in circles.

"MOM! Come out here!" Chris shouted from out front.

What now? Jamie shook her head, and opened the front door.

Chris, and Scott, one of his best buds; were bent down side by side on the shoveled walk. They could have been brothers. They had the same hair color, same posture, and same "we're up to something" grin.

"What's up, guys?"

Scott couldn't resist. "Hey, nice glove, Mrs. Stemple—starting a new trend?"

Chris ignored his comment, glanced behind him, and said, "Uh, Mom . . . remember when I told you about that adorable puppy who needed a home?"

"*And, Chris* . . . remember when I told you there's barely room for the four of us, let alone a dog?"

"But he's not a dog—he's just a puppy. See, look at him."

The boys stood up and moved aside. On the frozen concrete sat a shivering pup with short fur, a pencil tail, pouty brown eyes, and ears that didn't match: one stood up straight, and one turned down like a page in a good book.

Jamie walked down the steps, and the Labrador/Doberman puppy backed up on all fours, and growled at her with his mouth curled up to show little white teeth.

"Great, just what I need. Chris—"

"Mom, I'll take care of him—you won't have to do a thing—please?" He studied Jamie's face, and then added, "You don't want him dumped at the pound, do you?"

"Look at the size of those paws—he's going to be huge," Jamie said, bending down to reiterate paw size.

Big mistake. When Jamie looked into those eyes, and that little pencil tail started to wag, well . . . .

"So, what's his name?" she asked.

Chris and Scott looked at each other, and shrugged their shoulders. "Uh . . ." Chris began, "I don' know . . . I was just worried about getting him here."

Jamie shook her head. "He'll freeze out here—bring him inside . . . and I'll think about it."

"Okay. Thanks, Mom!"

Chris patted the top of Jamie's head, and gave the 'thumbs up' to Scott.

"Hey, Mom, what would *you* call him?"

Jamie looked at the little face. "If he were my dog, I'd name him "Rock.""

Chris and Scott looked at each other and nodded in agreement. "Rock. Rocky. I like it. Thanks, Mom!"

Like what?" Kayla asked, coming in the door behind them.

"My dog's name, 'Rock.'"

"Rocky—Like the movie—good choice." Kayla threw her backpack on the couch, and knelt down to meet the new family member. "He's so cute." Then in a whisper she added, "I knew Mom couldn't say no."

"I haven't said yes yet!" Jamie called from the kitchen.

"Come on, Scott, let's get something to eat," Chris said, and they boxed their way into the kitchen.

Jamie was quick. "Wait a minute. Back up, boys. Aren't you forgetting someone?"

"Oh, yeah," Chris said, spinning around, "I'll bet he's hungry too. Uh . . . Mom, do you have a couple bucks?"

"Two."

"Well, that'll buy him a little food."

After eating ham sandwiches and potato chips, the boys headed to the store. Jamie shook her head, and sat on the couch with Kayla.

"So how was your day?"

"It was fine," Kayla answered. "But how's your hand? I worried all day—and almost called you at lunch."

"Oh, it'll be all right," Jamie said, pretending it didn't hurt.

"You know, Mom . . . it's been a while since we hung out. What do you say we settle in with some of that spice tea you make—you know, with the Tang, spices and instant tea—I love that stuff."

"Sounds good to me."

At that moment, both the phone and doorbell rang. Kayla caught the phone, and Jamie opened the door to three lanky teenage boys.

"Hi, guys, if you're looking for Chris and Scott, they're down at Fred's Market."

"Okay, thanks," said the tallest of the group. And with their hands in their pockets, and the same long stride, they headed for the store.

Jamie closed the door, and Kayla thanked her friend for calling, but said she already had plans for the evening. She said goodbye, hung up the phone, and beat Jamie back to the sofa.

"Okay, now where were we?"

"You said something about tea?" Jamie asked with a smile."

"Yeah!" Kayla jumped up, and they headed for the kitchen, when the doorbell rang again.

"What *is* this?" Jamie turned around and went back to the front door.

"Yes?" she asked, rather abruptly.

A tall blonde man, probably late thirties, filled the doorway. "Jamie Stemple?"

"Uh . . . yes?"

"My name is Mark," he said in a clear Australian drawl. "A friend said you needed help with your car battery."

Jamie couldn't help but stare. "Uh . . . yes . . . uh . . . I'm sorry—I'm not used to this—I came from the city." *What a dumb thing to say.* "What I mean is . . . I can't pay you, I—"

"—No, that's not necessary," he said, holding up his hand. "I'm just here to help if I can. It is the battery, right?"

"Uh, yeah . . . ."

"Okay, let's go take a look." He looked at her gloved hand. "On second thought, why don't I go ahead and take care of it for you."

Kayla came up behind Jamie, and extended her hand. "Hi, I'm Kayla."

"Mark—nice to meet you."

Jamie continued to stare. "—Have you spent any time in Seattle? You look awfully familiar."

"Well now, that's kind of interesting. I have spent a bit of time there."

"Hmm. I'd swear we've met before."

"Well, I'd better check that battery," he said, and headed down the frozen walk.

"Thank you—I really appreciate this," Jamie said, as the wind kicked up.

"Not a problem," he said, and waved.

Jamie closed the door, and Kayla looked through the peephole.

"Geez, Mom, that's sure nice of him. And he's awfully cute."

"I know . . . but I don't get it. Who else knew about our car?"

Kayla shrugged. "Maybe one of Chris' friends. We should have asked him."

"Yeah, I will when he comes back to the door. And I know I've seen him somewhere before . . . hmm . . . well, come on, let's make some tea."

Once the water boiled, they carried steaming mugs back to the sofa. The fragrance of oranges, cloves, and something else filled the room.

"Kayla . . . it just dawned on me. I didn't see another car out front when Mark showed up. How's he going to charge the battery? And do you smell sage?"

Jamie set down her tea and opened the front door. The Buick's hood was down, and Mark was gone. She put on a coat, grabbed her keys, and slid in behind the wheel. Even using her left hand, the engine started right up.

"Hey, Riley, let's stop in Vantage for a little while."

"How about on the way home?" Riley answered, as the Columbia River came into view.

"*What?* We're at what should be called 'the archaeological capital of Washington,' and you don't want to stop?"

"I want to hear the rest of the story. And besides, isn't Grandpa Luke waiting for us?"

"Well, yeah." Kayla looked at her watch. "But we're ahead of schedule, and I really need to make a pit stop." She eased off the accelerator, exited the freeway, and turned left onto Vantage Highway.

The overpass gave a birds-eye view of I-90 as it crossed the river on the 2,504-foot long Vantage Bridge. Kayla took the first right, and headed down to the boat launch.

Riley frowned. "I thought you said, 'a pit stop?'"

"I did. But I want to read this sign."

They drove to the water's edge and pulled up to the white sign.

Riley frowned again. "Submerged hazards? Why doesn't it just say, 'Warning! Submerged town.'"

"That would work."

"Hmm . . . I wonder how much of old Vantage is still down there? It's been what—forty years?"

Before Kayla could answer, Riley continued. "Can you imagine, being told that after the dams are built, your town will be sitting at the bottom of the river?"

Kayla didn't attempt it, and Riley continued. "—I would love to meet someone who lived here back then. That amazes me. They chose to move their town—where do you find community spirit like that anymore?"

"I don't know, Riley . . . maybe in Adalon."

Back on Vantage Highway, they drove past the two gas stations, a cafe suitably named "Blustery's," a store called "The Store," and then turned right on Gingko Avenue.

Inside Ginkgo Petrified Forest State Park, they pulled up to a four-foot long chunk of wood. At first glance, the wood looked like that of any old waterlogged tree; and it was, until a chain of events caused it to change.

The nearby signboard, provided by the National Park Service, told the story of an ancient lake (along with another 63,000 miles) that filled with lava between twelve and seventeen million years ago. As the lava cooled around water soaked trees, the silica from the lava slowly replaced organic cells in the trees. Over time, the trees were transformed into "trees of stone."

Riley clapped her hands together. "Okay, let's get going—we don't want to be late."

"Don't you want to see the petroglyphs? They're right up your alley."

Kayla started down the asphalt path, but Riley didn't follow. She stayed by the sign, with her hands on her hips.

"Mom—come on! We can do this on the way home."

A family of five looked at Riley as they walked by. The parents smiled, and when they met Kayla on the path, the middle-aged dad said, "Usually it's the parent dragging the child back to the car."

Kayla nodded and went past. Then it hit her. She burst out laughing, ran past Riley, opened the car door, and yelled:

"Come on, Mom!"

Riley shook her head, and walked back to the car. "What was that all about, Mom?"

"Uh . . . I don't know what got into me."

"Maybe nothing . . . maybe it's the real you coming out."

Kayla frowned. And the brewing continued.

"Well, we know why these trees changed . . . but what changed you, Mom?

Silence.

"You know what I think, Mom? I think you used to be as curious as Grandma Jamie."

They backtracked to the freeway, and once again, Kayla was on a bridge looking out her side window, drawing strength from sun-kissed water.

They drove up the hill, past the wild horse monument, and Riley broke the silence again.

"Did you know there are really sixteen horses up on that ridge? Yep. One got tired of running, so he's lying down and won't get back up. Hmm . . . now who does that sound like?"

"You'll be a great archaeologist, Riley . . . you're awfully good at digging up the past."

Chapter Six

Chris and Scott came through the door like two bulls after a red flag.

"Man, I'm starving," Chris said and jerked open the refrigerator door. "Hmmp. We should have gone to your house, there's nothing in here."

Scott looked inside. "You got that right—what a bummer." He closed the door and looked around the floor. "Hey . . . where's your dog?"

"*My* dog? That's a laugh. He follows Mom everywhere. And when she makes him stay home, he shreds something—every time. Yesterday it was her dictionary, the day before that, the classifieds."

"Is she sick?"

Chris rifled through the cupboards. "Who? *Mom*? No—why would you ask that?"

"I heard that animals gravitate towards a person who's not well, that they have a sense about these things."

"Naah. Mom's fine—just a little uptight. So when does baseball start around here?"

"First part of March."

"Cool—that's in a week! Come on, let's go to your house," Chris said, and pushed Scott out of the kitchen.

"Where is your mom, anyways?"

"I don't know . . . hopefully at the store."

It took Jamie an hour to travel thirty-six miles to Breezley—the nearest town with more than one grocery store. Roads were slick, with drop-offs up to eight feet between the road and wheat fields. And with drifting snow, it was difficult to see where the road ended and the fields began.

She spent the morning talking herself in and out of the trip, so when she arrived at the two-story Breezley Inn, she searched for strength just to get through the door.

Once inside, she sat in the pastel lobby and filled out the generic application. After signing her name at the bottom—stating that everything written was true—she attached her resume, handed it to the perky young clerk, and tried to exit gracefully.

Good thing it didn't say: "By signing, you know in your heart you should do this."

Between the headache she woke up with, and the frustration of job-hunting, Jamie was ready to throw up as she drove out of town. *What am I suppose to do? It's been six months.*

The only sound was the hum of studded tires on a frozen highway.

Everywhere was white. Like one long, continuous cotton sheet. Without the intermittent farms, it would've been impossible to distinguish between land and sky. A white sky was a snow sky; and in whiteout conditions, this could make for a long, spooky drive home.

Jamie came to the sign for Hawkins Road, and remembered seeing the same sign on Camas Hill Road—the road into Adalon. It made sense that if she jumped on Hawkins Road from here, it would save time; instead of driving another five miles to Camas Hill Road, and then up another eight to the point where the roads intersect. *After all, the shortest distance between two points is a straight line.*

So she made a slippery left-hand turn, and barreled down what felt like a toboggan run.

A few miles into it, the road split in an unforeseen "y" and Jamie veered left, thinking it was headed north to Adalon. The narrow road wound up a hill, cornered to the right, then a sharp left.

Oh, no!

In front of her was an unmarked four-way intersection. Jamie stopped in the middle and looked down each way. There were a few homes in the distance, but she couldn't tell if the roads leading to them were thoroughfares or private drives. She chose a right turn, drove about half a mile, and dead-ended in front of three

German Shepherds—who took their job of guarding the farm very seriously.

Jamie turned around as fast as she could, sped back to the intersection, and took a right. Deserted homesteads were easy to spot. They were the ones circled in snow, and frozen in time—no lights, no power lines, no plowed driveways. But for the most part, everywhere looked the same: miles of white fields and snow-packed gravel roads. The more times she turned around, the more she lost her bearings.

It was dusk. It was snowing. And her great shortcut had eaten up an hour and most of her gasoline. Jamie stopped the car and smacked the steering wheel with her fist.

"Why do I do these things?" she said aloud, and took a deep breath. "Okay, don't panic, this maze can't last forever." She looked in all directions for the lights of Adalon. "Father, please show me the way home."

She turned the heater up a notch, let her foot off the brake, and grit her teeth as the wheels spun on ice. After a while, she rounded a right corner, and then a left, wound down a hill, and came to back to the "y" in the road. Jamie leaned back in the seat and closed her eyes. "Thank you, Father."

Immediately, the golden eagle appeared in front of her, and the snow stopped falling. He blinked at her and then soared to the left.

Jamie opened her eyes. The snow *had* stopped falling, and the air smelled of sage. *And the eagle?* She wanted to turn left . . . but was afraid, and turned right instead, retracing her steps back to familiar territory.

Luke made it home late Friday night; and by Saturday afternoon, the wallpaper was closing in on them.

"Come on," Luke said, "let's go to Breezley. I need some parts for the truck."

Around town, icicles were melting; and from Camas Hill Road, they could see a change in the wheat fields. On Monday the fields were glossed in white, like meringue on top of a lemon pie; and today, green blades of winter wheat poked through.

Luke found the parts he needed at Western Auto, and all too soon they were headed back to Adalon.

"I've been thinking about our situation, James . . . and until you're working, we can't do much of anything. We'll just have to sit tight for a while."

Jamie didn't answer. What could she say? It was true.

"So . . . have you been looking? Do you have any leads yet?"

"Nothing concrete," she said, hoping he would drop it. But he didn't.

"You're still writing, aren't you?"

She glanced at the upcoming sign. "Luke, turn left here!"

"What for?"

"I want to see something."

"What?"

"Uh . . . there's an entrance to this road on Camas Hill, so it must connect—and I want to see what's down here. It's not like it's out of our way."

"Let me guess. You were out exploring again, weren't you? And you didn't answer my other question, so I'll take that as a yes."

Jamie avoided his eyes.

"I know you, James. And someday, you're going to get yourself in a predicament, and not be able to get yourself out of it."

If he only knew . . . .

They came to the "y" and Jamie quickly said, "Stay to the right."

"Okay, but don't get us both lost."

Jamie studied the terrain as it begun to change. The fields sloped downward, and basalt rocks jutted out in the distance. The farther they went, the more apparent the basalt walls were. Jamie's heart quickened as she felt the place they were headed to.

The road was slick, but nothing like Monday. They continued downward, driving along a variegated brown wall, and then around a sharp corner to the left. The view was blocked by another rock wall, and as they got closer to seeing around it, Jamie could hardly breathe.

"I don't know, James, are you sure this connects?"

"Yes—keep going!"

Luke looked over at her. "Are you okay?"

"I'm fine—"

Even in the snow she recognized it. It *was* real. And it *was* splendid.

"Wow!" Luke said, slowing down the truck. "It's beautiful!"

Neither of them could take their eyes off the land.

"Do you smell that, Luke?"

"Smell what?"

"Sage."

"Jamie, it's still winter . . . you can't smell sage in the winter."

A white '75 AMC Pacer came around the corner, turned into the property, and stopped.

"Must be the owner," Luke said.

Jamie slumped down in the seat, then shot back up a moment later.

It was real. It was splendid. And at that moment, was being posted for sale.

They looked at each other with that 'we shouldn't, but let's ask anyways' look, and got out of the truck. The tall lady with turquoise jewelry and long, silver-streaked, dark hair, smiled as they approached.

"Hi there! Beautiful view, huh?"

"Sure is," Luke said. "How many acres?"

"Two hundred and eighty." She held out her hand. I'm Erika Parks."

They shook hands, and she continued. "Peculiar place, though . . . ."

"How so?" Jamie asked.

"It's never been settled. Since the early 1900s many have tried, but they were all unsuccessful. I don't know what it is . . . but this place seems to have a heartbeat of its own . . . almost like it's waiting for someone."

Jamie almost fell over.

Luke frowned. "Sounds like a legend to me."

"I suppose it does. But I've posted this land six times in the last nine years—and every time, the owners relinquished it back."

"Why?" Jamie asked, trying to contain herself.

"Various reasons. One couldn't make the payments, one said the wind made his wife crazy; another one said it was the dust, another was afraid of snakes, and so on and so on.

After a long pause, Luke asked about price and terms. And that's where the discussion ended.

"Well," Luke said, "there's no point in wasting your time. It's way out of our range—but thank you for the information, it was . . . interesting."

Luke turned to leave, and Jamie had to force her feet to move. She knew what was around that outcropping of rocks; but she asked anyways.

"Erika, I'm curious . . . on the other side of those rocks, is there a steep mesa standing alone in the coulee? And that small lake over there—" she asked quickly, pointing to the right, "is it shaped like a heart?"

"Right on both accounts . . . so you've been here before."

Jamie turned to look at Luke who was already at the truck, "In a way . . . well it's nice meeting you."

Jamie walked back to the truck, and they both took one more look before heading on to Adalon.

"That was strange stuff she was saying."

Jamie nodded, and stared out the window. "I never realized that sage changes with the seasons. Look at the leaves. The tips have turned gold.

Back at the little house, Luke changed spark plugs in the truck, and Jamie pulled out her journal and smiled.

The land wasn't mentioned for the rest of the week-end, and Sunday evening, the three stood on the porch as Luke drove away. He'd planned to leave early Monday morning, but a surprise snowfall changed that.

Father, please watch over Luke, and keep him safe for me.

Chris went inside and grabbed his basketball. "Bye. I'm gonna shoot some hoops."

"It's snowing! And what about your homework?"

"Very observant, Mom, and my homework *is* done." He patted Jamie on the head, and bounced his ball down the white street.

"So Kayla, what are you doing tonight?"

Kayla stood in front of the TV, turning the channel knob. "I was going to watch *The Nancy Drew Mysteries*. It's suppose to be on Sundays at seven, but it's not."

"Well, maybe it's pre-empted. Anyways, there's something I'm dying to tell you."

"Cool! I'm all ears." Kayla turned off the TV, and they sat on opposite ends of the couch, with their feet in the middle.

"Okay," Jamie took a deep breath, and then frowned. "I don't know where to start."

"Uh—the beginning?"

"Okay . . . the very beginning." Jamie repositioned herself, and began. "I was born on June 1, 1942; the same day water first poured over spillway gates at Grand Coulee Dam. As a kid I was fascinated by this, so on my thirteenth birthday I asked my folks for a trip to the dam. I think that shocked them. But I guess I've always been a little different."

Kayla smirked.

"Anyways, they granted my wish, and we journeyed to North Central Washington to see the largest concrete dam in North America. But when we got there, I realized it wasn't the dam, but the basalt walls of the Grand Coulee itself, that fascinated me. And that was clear back in 1955."

Jamie hesitated, and Kayla pushed her feet. "Come on—I know there's a punch line here."

Jamie pulled her legs up to her knees, and proceeded with the current events, starting with the dream she had when they first moved over.

"Mom, this is crazy!"

"I know . . . but then, so was moving to Adalon."

Chapter Seven

*J*amie stared out the window and gulped the last of her morning coffee. *Winter is finally over . . . and spring has never felt like this before.* She pondered a moment longer, then checked the time.

"Bye, guys, I have to get going."

Chris appeared, rubbing his hair with a towel. "How do you get up so early when I hear you typing in the middle of the night? What are you working on?"

Jamie hesitated. "I'm still trying to sell one of my stories . . . anyways, I—"

"Mom, wait!" Kayla yelled, and stumbled around the corner. "What time will you be home? I need a ride to the game."

"I should be back by three."

"Maybe—if you don't stop on Hawkins Road," Chris said, and patted the top of her head.

"No, today I'll just drive by." Jamie pulled him in for a hug and kissed his cheek. Have a great day, okay?"

"Yeah, right . . . school's boring," he said, and walked towards the door.

"Hey, there's going to be a rodeo here Memorial Day weekend—that could be fun."

"Yeah, right . . . bye, Mom."

After filling out four applications, driving about eighty miles, and smiling more than she felt like; Jamie headed home, via Hawkins Road of course. But when she drove around the rock wall, the sign was gone.

"No! It can't be sold."

Jamie sped back to Adalon, and rushed in the house. After finding the phone number, she took a deep breath and dialed.

"Erika Parks, please!" she blurted out when someone answered; then pushed on the back of her head, trying to make the pain stop. A moment later Erika came on the line.

"Hi, this is Erika."

"—This is Jamie Stemple—I don't know if you remember me, we met a few months ago—"

"Hi, Jamie, of course I remember. How are you?"

"—What happened to the land? The sign's gone."

"It sold . . . the deal closed yesterday."

"—No, it can't! I—we . . . never mind . . . I'm sorry to bother you." Jamie hung up the phone, and slumped down in the chair.

On Friday night, Luke came home four hours early, which put him in the door right before sunset.

"James, let's go for a drive."

"*What?* You've been on the road for four hours, and you want to get back in the truck. Why?"

"Just come with me, okay? There's something I need to do."

Jamie took two more aspirin and grabbed her jean jacket.

As they approached Hawkins Rd, Jamie closed her eyes, and Luke let off the accelerator.

"Let's take the shortcut."

"No, let's not."

"Come on, James. I want to see that property again."

"Why? It's sold."

"So . . . it's still nice to look at."

"Luke—I don't want to see it."

"Oh, come on . . . you know you do."

Jamie pretended to look out her window; but her eyes were closed. It didn't matter though; she still pictured every detail. And when Luke stopped at the gate, she felt a clunk in her heart.

"Let's go for a walk."

"Luke, it's private property. We can't just 'go for a walk.'"

"The new owners won't mind—they're really cool."

Luke jumped out, and hustled around to Jamie's door. She slid out of the truck, and Luke towed her through the weathered gate.

It was sunset. A rose hue splashed across tall basalt walls. The talus slopes and coulee floor were bright with new grass, fresh sage, dots of purple and white lupine, and the air was filled with sage perfume.

They followed the road past the outcropping of rocks, and Jamie winced at the mesa she already knew.

"It's beautiful, huh?" Luke said. "Kind of shaped like a giant six-story Aussie hat."

"Let's go, Luke."

"Don't you want to meet the new owners?"

"No! *Why?*"

"I told you, they're really cool."

"I don't care how cool they are, I don't want to meet them—and I don't want to be out here—so can we please leave?"

Luke held out his hand.

"Luke—what are you doing?" She kicked a few rocks to hide her expression.

He grabbed her hand, and turned her towards him.

"Jamie . . ." he said while shaking her hand. "Hello. My name is Luke Stemple—"

"Come on, Luke, knock it off."

He ignored her, and continued. "And I must be totally insane; because my wife, and two kids and I . . . are now the proud owners of this fine place . . ." he paused, and looked around, ". . . of rocks and sagebrush."

"That's not funny, Luke."

She pushed his hand away, but stared in his eyes. When Luke teased her, his eyes danced like little stars, and couldn't hold a stare. But they weren't dancing, and his sapphire blues held up to her greens.

"That's just—not funny—you shouldn't tease me about something like this. I love this land—and I know it's suppose to be ours—" she rubbed tears away with her sleeve, "this isn't a good joke."

"Who's joking? It *is* ours."

"*What?*" she asked, as the tears continued. "You're serious? But how—I thought—" she threw her arms around him, and screamed in his ear.

"Hold on, James. Before you get too excited . . . there's a big condition we have to talk about." He unwrapped her arms from around his neck, and held her hands.

"There's a huge balloon payment due one year from the closing date, which would be May 15, 1978. I figure we can swing it, if we can get a house built—almost to completion, and then refinance the entire package into one mortgage. It's the only way—we only have a year, it won't be easy, and I can't do it alone . . . what do you think?"

"I think I love you."

"Well I think we're crazy. But, if we push hard enough, I think we can do it. But, it means four things: you need a job today, I'll have to stay in Seattle for another year, we have to do all the work ourselves, and we'll be financially tapped until it's over. So do you still love me?"

"More than ever." She hugged him again, and tears fell on his shoulder.

They continued walking down towards the lake, and Jamie was ready to burst.

"Luke, I have to ask. What made you do it?"

79

"Are you kidding—this place haunted me. And I knew you fell in love with it."

Before Jamie could respond, his tone dropped.

"But James, you've got to keep your promise."

"I know . . . and I will," she said, as three little words hovered in her mind.

Place . . . of . . . sage.

Chapter Eight

September 6, 1977:

There's a reason God brought us to this side of the
mountain. There's a reason He guided us to this
piece of land. There's a reason I've dreamt of being
a writer—and feel such urgency to do so. And there's
a reason things don't make sense. I just wish I knew
what all these reasons were. I have a feeling they all
tie together . . . and that's what scares me.

*J*amie closed the soft black cover, and tucked
the journal away.

At daybreak, combines that cut wheat, tractors with
drills for planting wheat, and trucks that haul wheat;
rumbled down Main Street. Harvest was wrapping up,
and the rush was on to get seed wheat planted, and
sprouted, before the rain came.

If it rained, and then the ground warmed back up, the top layer of soil would crust over, and young wheat is not strong enough to break through it.

Hmm . . . I guess I have learned a few things.

"Morning, Mom."

"Hey, Punkin, how are you?"

Kayla rolled her eyes. "I can't believe school's starting again."

"I know . . . and I can't believe you're in driver's Ed. already."

"Yeah . . . I can finally drive."

Jamie sipped her coffee and smiled. "God has great things planned for my kids."

"You think so?"

"I know so."

"How?"

Jamie glanced at the clock on the wall. "Another time, you've got to get ready for school."

Kayla walked to the bedroom door, and turned to look at Jamie. "Must be the same way I know, that you're gonna be a great writer." She twirled around and went in her room.

Chris wolfed down his Wheaties, and watched Rock follow Jamie from one room, to another, and then to the kitchen.

"Uh, Mom . . . are you feeling all right?"

Jamie opened the cupboard containing aspirin, and then closed it when she looked at Chris.

"What do you mean?"

Kayla heard the question, and popped her head out the bedroom door. "What he means is, you take way too much aspirin, and you always have a headache."

In between bites, Chris mumbled, "No . . . I didn't know about the headaches. Actually, it was something I heard about dogs, and this theory—" He looked at Kayla, who was about to laugh. "—Oh never mind."

"You guys, I'm fine. But thanks for caring."

Kayla ran in to get dressed, and Chris put his bowl in the sink.

"Mom, maybe you should see a doctor. Just to be sure."

After they left, Jamie opened the cupboard, and got out two aspirin. She leaned against the sink, and wondered what theory Chris was talking about. The phone rang as she finished the glass of water.

"Hello?"

From the other end of the line came, "Hello . . . I'm trying to reach Luke or Jamie Stemple."

Great, another solicitor. "This is Jamie."

"Okay—good. My name is Sam Andrews. I'm an archaeologist for the Bureau of Land Management, and I'm working on a land swap between the Bureau and the D.N.R."

"D.N.R.? What's that?"

"Oh, I'm sorry—Department of Natural Resources. I need to run surveys on the state land adjacent from your property on Hawkins Rd . . . and I was wondering if it'd be okay if I accessed the parcel from your land. I'd hike in and be careful not to disrupt anything. And if this was possible, I was thinking of tomorrow morning."

"Well . . . sure, I don't see any problem in that. Maybe I could tag along, I'll probably be out there anyways."

"Uh . . . that'd be great . . . tomorrow then, say . . . uh . . . eight A.M."

"Okay. Do you need directions?"

Without hesitation, Sam answered, "No—I know where it is . . . I love that area . . . and thank you . . . uh . . . so . . . I guess I'll . . . see you in the morning. Oh—let me give you my number in case something comes up . . ."

Jamie jotted the number on a tablet, hung up, and thought that was one of the strangest phone calls she'd had in a while. At first he was articulate and businesslike, but by the end of the call, he was almost stuttering.

The day was filled with phone calls. Some good, and some not. Chris was getting in trouble at school, and Jamie was summoned to a meeting with the principal; her check for the building permit bounced; and later when Kayla walked in, she was on the phone with Luke.

"I know—I'll handle it, and I'll call you after the meeting . . . I already called the bank . . . yes, of course I'm looking . . . no, I haven't heard anything from the inn."

Kayla yelled a "Hi Dad, I love you!" and headed for the refrigerator.

A few minutes later, Jamie came in the kitchen. "Dad said Hi, and he loves you too."

"What's wrong, Mom?"

"Nothing . . . do you want to go down to the property with me? Dad thought he left the tool shed unlocked."

"Mom, don't lie to me. I can tell when something's bothering you."

"I know you can."

Kayla sat on the counter, and Jamie leaned against the sink.

"It's just that, every time I go job hunting, I have this sick feeling in my stomach that it's wrong. But how can that be—I promised I would. I have to! We can't afford to live if I don't, and Dad will never get moved over."

Jamie took a deep breath, and shook her head.

"And I hear God say, "Keep writing." How stupid is that? I'm a writing flop! And don't say anything—you asked. Oh, and there's more. There's this name that keeps rolling around in my head. And when I'm working on a story, I'll type it in without realizing it. But I can't use it, because I can't see her face . . . just a name."

"What is it?" Kayla asked, when Jamie didn't offer.

"'Teri.' I even dreamt about her once. I know—call the men in white suits. Anyways, in my dream, she was standing in this wide-open place with her back towards me. She had long blond hair, and was wearing a long dark coat. For a moment, everything was still. Then I heard a man yell her name . . . I remember it echoed. And as she turned around . . . I woke up. Never seeing her face."

"That's pretty wild, Mom."

"Yeah . . . it is, huh? Well come on—let's head on down."

Luke was right. Wind had blown the shed door open, and blue plastic tarps were scattered about the home site. One was stuck to rebar on the foundation footings, another clung to a pile of two-by-fours, one blew under the portable shed, and two were out in the sage.

Jamie headed for the sage; and Kayla bent down to retrieve the tarp under the shed. She couldn't quite reach it, so she got down on her hands and knees, and was about to lean down and grab the plastic, when Jamie shouted:

"Kayla, come here!"

Kayla scrambled to her feet and rushed over in concern.

"What's wrong?"

Jamie studied a long, winged, green creature sitting on the tarp. "Have you ever really looked at a dragonfly? What does he remind you of?"

"You called me over here to see a bug?"

"Well yeah. Look at him. Do you think that's where the idea for helicopters came from?

"Oh brother."

"I'm serious, Kayla—look. It's the same design."

Kayla nodded her infamous "yeah right, Mom" and headed for the tarp on the woodpile.

After following the dragonfly a few yards, Jamie looked up and noticed the tarps folded in a neat pile. She jumped up, and raced Kayla for the last tarp, under the shed.

"I'll get it—you picked up all the rest."

Jamie was in old clothes, so she didn't hesitate to plop down on the dirt and reach under the shed. She grabbed the end of the plastic, and—

"STOP!" He said.

She froze, and her eyes shot to the right as the end of a snake slid under the plastic.

In slow motion, Jamie let go of the tarp, and scooted backwards to a distance she felt safe enough to stand up, turn around, and run.

"Kayla, get in the car!"

"Just a minute, I have to put these in the shed."

"No! Just leave them—I mean it—get in the car!"

Kayla dropped the tarps, and watched Jamie throw several fist-sized rocks on them. Then she spun around, grabbed a two-by-four, used the end to push the shed door closed, dropped it, and ran back to the car.

"Mom, what are you doing?"

"There's a rattlesnake under there!"

Jamie was jumping in place and shaking her hands. "Do you realize you could've been bitten? I would never have forgiven myself—oh, God, thank you! What would I have done?"

"Mom, are you sure it was a rattlesnake?"

Jamie was still jumping. "It had rattles—of course I'm sure!"

"Well, what do we do? How do we get it out of there?"

"I don't know. I'm from the city—what do I know about deadly snakes."

They both looked at the shed, and shivered.

That night, Jamie spread her blanket on the sofa, and closed the blinds just enough to see the cross. *Thank you, Father, for being there today.*

At two o'clock, the pain woke her from a deep sleep. This was a first. She staggered out to the kitchen for aspirin, and then crawled back into bed.

She stayed perfectly still, hoping the pain would stop; and her first inclination was that she was hearing things—due to the fact that her head felt like it was caught in a giant vice grip. But she knew that voice, and His voice was uncompromising.

"Keep writing. A breakthrough is coming."

Naturally, her next thought was, *Writing what?* She had collected more story rejection letters in the last eight months, than she had the entire fifteen years before that. How many was that? More fingers than she had hands for. But still, she knew . . . that when God of the entire universe gives you a job to do . . . you better do it.

"I trust you, Father," she whispered. "But what on earth am I going to say to Luke? I promised him." Tears slid by her ear, and onto her pillow.

The next morning, sunlight peeked through the blinds, and Jamie woke to the sound of children on the street. She sprung out of bed—this wasn't her normal wake up sound. Of course not, it was seven-thirty.

"Kayla, Chris, wake up! We're late!"

In a race for the shower, four feet hit the floor, and two doors slammed shut.

Jamie threw on jeans, a T-shirt, and frowned in the mirror. She plunked a ball cap on her head and knocked on the bathroom door.

"Grab a towel, I'm coming in—sorry."

"Mom!"

Chris scrambled for a towel, and jumped behind the shower curtain.

"Sorry, but I'm suppose to be at the property in ten minutes to meet that archaeologist."

Chris poked his head out of the shower. "*What?* Alone? I don't like that idea."

"I won't be alone, the well driller's out there," Jamie said while simultaneously brushing her teeth and applying deodorant.

"I still don't like it."

"Chris, I'll be fine. I want to see where the property boundaries are; and besides, I've never met an archaeologist."

With the kids set for the day, Jamie and Rock flew out the door. It was easy to speed on Camas Hill Rd, but not so on Hawkins. She quickly learned that turning a corner on gravel, while speeding, didn't work well.

Hopefully the archaeologist is late, too.

But, much to her dismay, when she came down the hill and turned the last corner, he was standing in front of the gate. She pulled up in a dust plume, and the tall Indian man, with shoulder length hair, tried not to laugh.

"Great," she mumbled, and pulled the hat over her eyes.

He walked over to the Buick as Jamie opened the door, but when she looked up at him, he stopped suddenly. After an awkward pause, Jamie held out her hand.

"Hi, I'm Jamie . . . you must be Sam."

He hesitated, then instead of shaking her hand, he held on to it.

Jamie felt the delay, and looked at his hand. It was large and calloused, with the scars of hard work. It reminded her of Luke's hand, and she liked him for that. She realized, though, that too many seconds had passed, and pulled her hand away.

"Uh, nice to meet you, Jamie . . . and thank you—for letting me do this. It'll shave about two hours off my hike."

"Thanks for letting me tag along."

Jamie studied his eyes. They were dark, with crinkles one gets from squinting in the sun. But there was something about them . . . and when he caught her scrutiny, he quickly looked away.

He bent down to meet Rock—who liked him right away. She wasn't surprised, so did she.

The well driller, who reminded her of a lumberjack, waved as they pulled up to the site. And while Sam gathered up his equipment, Jamie strolled over to inquire about her new well.

"How far are you? Any sign of water yet?" she yelled, over the "thump, thump, thump" of the drill.

"No water at a hundred feet."

"Ugh, this isn't good—is it?"

Chapter Eight

"Well, could be better. But there's an aquifer under here. We just have to reach it."

"A what?"

"Aquifer—a layer of underground sand and gravel where water collects—like an underground river."

Jamie thought about that for a moment, and Sam walked over, slinging a backpack over his shoulder.

"Just a few more feet, huh?"

Jamie tried not to laugh when the driller gave him the 'how would you know?' look.

"Well, shall we go?"

"Uh . . . yeah," Sam said, still watching the operation.

They headed north through the sage, and Rock darted in and out, and around every bush he could.

"You need to watch him, Jamie. There are holes he should stay away from, and he shouldn't be poking around rocks unsupervised. He could surprise a rattler, a porcupine, a badger—now there's a mean critter, you should see their claws. Have you noticed any holes the size of a basketball, that go down at an angle? Badgers."

"Great," Jamie said, as Rock rustled up a sagebrush full of chukars, and then took off after a rabbit.

"So, Sam . . . what kind of Indian are you?"

"What *kind*?"

"Your . . . affiliation—your tribe."

Sam smiled. "The Lakota."

The sage was blooming, and Jamie picked an armful of stems in shades of pink, white, yellow and orange. Rock scouted the trail in front of them, and for a while, the only sounds were grasshoppers jumping through dry grass, their boots as they brushed by sage, and the red-tailed hawk overhead.

Jamie felt small as they walked between the tall columnar walls that defined the coulee.

"So, Sam . . . are you married? Any kids?"

"I have a wife," Sam answered without looking at her. "And I have a son, he's seventeen this year. His name is Shep.

"Have you always lived here?"

"No . . . I was raised in South Dakota . . ." he paused a moment. "I moved out here sixteen years ago."

"Why, what brought you clear out here?"

"You ask a lot of questions, don't you?"

Something in his eyes changed, and he stopped walking.

"I'm sorry, I didn't mean to pry."

"No . . . I'm the one who's sorry," he said looking at the coulee wall. "I'm going to have to do this another day."

"Sam, I'm sorry . . . did I offend you?"

"It's not you. And I didn't mean to drag you out here for nothing." He looked down at the ground. "But I'll take care of that snake before I go."

Jamie flinched and looked down. "What snake?"

"The one that frightened you."

Sam headed towards the home site, as if he couldn't get away from her fast enough. Jamie and Rock looked at each other.

"How did you know about that snake?" She yelled, and then dashed to catch up with him. And when she did, he wouldn't look at her face.

"The same way I know that when your spirit soars, you play "Edelweiss" on your flute, on that mesa top."

"And how do you know that? We just met."

"This is not the time, Jamie."

"Time for what? Wait a minute."

Sam stopped walking. After another moment of silence, he said, "Your flute is on the front seat of your car, right? Maybe I just assumed you play your music up there."

"Okay—maybe . . . that is the only thing that makes sense—seeing how I've only known you for about an hour now."

He refused to look at her eyes. "Jamie, if you'll give me a few moments alone, we'll rid you of the rattle-snakes; and they won't bother you again."

We?

They returned to the site. He set down his backpack, and headed for the shed, and Jamie walked a wide half-circle to watch.

Sam pulled sage leaves from the branches and rubbed them in his hands. Then, after circling the shed, he knelt down on his knees about six feet away, and began to pray. It was not a language Jamie understood, but she wished she did, it was beautiful. With fists of pungent sage, he held his arms in the air.

Within minutes, the snake slithered out from under the shed, and came within three feet of him. Jamie couldn't believe what she was seeing. The snake coiled up tight, and the rattle was a sound she would never forget.

Seconds went by. Sam continued to pray.

Finally, he stood up in one balanced movement and let the sage fall from his hands. In a single motion, he stepped towards the snake with his arm extended forward and hand cupped downward, grabbed the snake below the head, and flung it in the air.

In an instant, flapping golden wings blocked the sun. The eagle swooped down, grabbed the snake with its talons, and disappeared.

The only evidence that what just happened, really did happen, was the feather floating to the ground between them. Sam picked it up, gently blew the dust off and handed it to Jamie.

"Follow the eagle. He will lead you home."

She started to tell him about the golden eagle, but he held up his hand, and nodded. "I know. And the time for understanding will come."

Jamie didn't move. Neither did the well driller who, even from a distance, wore the same puzzled expression.

While in prayer, Sam collected more leaves, walked the perimeters of the home site, and smudged with sage the four directions. After that, he put a smudge on Jamie's forehead.

"You're safe out here. The Creator protects you."

He then walked past the well driller who repositioned his stance and said, "two more feet then?"

"Yes," Sam answered, without stopping. He reached his rig, threw in his backpack, and then turned to look at Jamie.

Jamie stared with the feather in hand, as he came back over. He put his hand on the back of her head, and for a moment she thought she saw tears.

"Jamie . . . you have a portion of my heart. So I must say to you . . . don't ignore this pain any longer."

Chapter Nine

Jamie and Rock stood on top of their mesa. "Father, what do I do? There's no time."

The wall of water thundered through the coulee, tossing boulders, dwarfing the four-hundred-foot high basalt wall, and submerging everything in its path.

Luke, Chris, and Kayla were safe on top of the wall; but there was no time for Jamie and Rock.

"Father, please help us!"

She looked down, and the Lord appeared, on the ground between them and the approaching water.

"Do you trust Me, Jamie?"

"Yes, but—"

He held His hand out to her. "Then come down and stand by Me."

"No—the water!"

"You said you trust Me."

She screamed out in anguish; then hurried over the steep edge, knocking rocks loose, slipping, bruising her knees, and cutting her hands.

"Rock, come on!" she yelled, as he hesitated on the jagged ledge. "Hurry!"

Finally they were down. With the raging water about to engulf them, she bolted to the Lord and grabbed His hand.

The water stopped instantly.

It was still there.

It still roared.

But it was still.

The wall of water didn't move.

Jamie gulped a breath of air, and sat up. It was two A.M. She scrambled for her journal and pen. After writing every detail, she stepped out on the porch to calm down. The cross glowed, and the harvest moon of September had changed to the crescent moon of mid October.

Jamie tried to analyze what the dream meant, and how it tied in with everything else—because she knew it did . . . somehow. But after a few minutes, her skin turned cold, and she went inside.

Saturday morning, Luke paced back and forth and stared at his watch.

"Where is that backhoe? I told them I needed it by eight."

"It'll be here," Jamie said.

"When? It's ten o'clock! I've lost three hours of daylight already. I've got two days to dig three hundred feet of trench, and lay all the power, septic and water lines—how am I supposed to do that without a back-hoe—and where's Chris? I told him to get here early."

Jamie and Kayla looked at each other.

"He'll be here," Jamie said. "What can we work on?"

"I don't know—it's going to start raining, and then we'll be working in a mud bog." He leaned on the shovel. "What was I thinking? Two days a week isn't cutting it—we'll never get this place sealed up by winter!"

"We have to try, Luke."

"What do you think I'm doing here? I am trying! And what about you?"

He threw the shovel and walked towards the shed. She got the point.

Chris arrived right before the backhoe.

"Sorry, Mom, I had to wait for Scott's dad, to get a ride down here."

"Well, I'm glad you're here now."

"Is Dad mad?"

"He has a lot on his mind."

The sky changed from fluffy white cumulus clouds, to the low gray nimbus full of rain; and in short order, dry, dusty air turned to a blend of wet dirt and sage.

By day's end, the sage was a dark green-gray, trenches were caving in, and the Stemples were soaked.

By the end of the weekend, the site looked like a war zone for giant moles; and mud was deep enough to swallow their feet. But, all the lines were in place, and they were ready for the inspectors.

Luke said goodbye, again, and Jamie closed the door to the little house.

Father, please keep him safe for me.

Chris and Kayla went in their rooms, and Jamie had the evening to work.

You keep telling me to write, and I keep trying. So why can't I sell a single story?

The next morning, Jamie's head and neck ached more than usual. She thought about what Sam had said, and when the kids left for school, she phoned the clinic in Breezley.

"Is this an emergency?" the receptionist asked.

"I hope not," Jamie replied.

They set the appointment for ten o'clock on Thursday; and Jamie got on with her day.

She didn't want to get the mail, but knew she had to; so she drove two blocks to the post office, hoping to get in and out, and not have to talk to anyone. Not so. As she was going in, Milly Edwards was coming out.

"Jamie Stemple . . . where have you been? I haven't seen you for months."

"I know. A lot's happened."

Jamie moved out of the doorway to let a few people in, and Milly smiled as they said "good morning."

"So . . . has that man of yours moved over yet?"

"No, it's going to be a while . . ."

"Yeah, I bet. I heard about the place you bought."

"Of course you did," Jamie said, moving out of the way again.

Milly squeezed her hand, and smiled. "Hon, I wish I could stay and chat, but I've got sourdough bread rising. And I'm still waiting for that long story of yours."

"Thanks, Milly . . . it's good to see you—I'm sorry it's been so long."

"It has, huh? Before you know it, it's going to be Christmas again."

"Yeah . . . well maybe this year I can put a tree on *your* doorstep."

Milly waved goodbye, and stepped out on the street. She stopped where the centerline would be, if there were one, and turned around.

"Jamie!"

Jamie turned and looked out the door.

"Keep writing!" Milly shouted.

Jamie waved, and noticed the faces watching them. *The things you learn at the post office.* She turned the key in her box and pulled out the usual assortment of junk mail and bills—mostly bills. *Great, and Thursday I'll add another one to the stack.*

Before she knew it, it *was* Thursday. Jamie walked out of the clinic with a headache, and the same information she had going in. None. Her test results would be back next week, so for now, she waited.

Luke came home late Friday night; and early Saturday morning, all family members were present to start on the framing. Luke sifted through the two-by-fours, Jamie poured coffee from a thermos, Kayla fidgeted with her jacket, and Chris stared up at the coulee wall.

"We've been studying this in social studies," Chris said. "Did you know these rocks were made from lava a million years ago? And then, during the Ice Age, an ice dam broke over in Montana, and for a couple thousand years, giant walls of water and ice carved out these cou- lees. Wow! Think about it. If that were to ever happen again, we'd be right in the middle of the flood!

"That's it!"

Jamie jumped, and looked at Luke. "What?"

"At the price we paid for these boards—they could at least be straight! Half of them are garbage."

Chris and Kayla looked at each other, and took a few steps backwards.

"Geez, Chris, that's pretty good, all that history stuff. Since when do *you* pay attention at school?"

"Well, it was interesting."

Luke tossed aside another board, walked over to his truck, and leaned into the bed.

Jamie went and stood beside him. "So . . . where's your barn going to go?"

"*What* barn? It's not going to happen."

"Yes it is, Luke . . . you'll have a ranch, you'll see."

"*Yeah?* All I see is a disaster. We've used up our sav- ings, maxed out our credit cards—hell, we were broke last month—and we don't even have walls yet! But why should I care—you don't!"

"Of course I do."

"Right . . . if you did, you'd have a job by now. That *was* the promise—remember?"

"Of course I remember . . . but God knows what he's doing."

"*GOD?* We're the ones working our butts off here, not God! This isn't a fairy tale, James. Here in the real world, if we miss our deadline, we lose everything."

Luke got in the truck, and peeled out down the driveway. Jamie kicked a rock and looked down the coulee. *Getting a job would be much easier.* She took a deep breath, and thought for sure she heard rushing water.

"I do trust you, Father," she whispered.

Rock started barking, and Chris pointed across the canyon. "Mom—look! There are two guys down there."

"What?"

"By the lake, over by that old homestead. And it looks like they have guns."

Jamie focused on the fluorescent orange vests. "That's right . . . I heard something about hunting season. Great! And your Dad just left."

Chris crossed his arms. "Well, we better do something—they're on our property."

"Okay, you guys wait here—"

"Oh yeah—right, Mom," Kayla said. "We're gonna let you go over there by yourself."

"I don't think so," Chris said, and straightened his shoulders. "Come on, let's go."

Kayla and Jamie smiled at each other as they marched out across the sage. The hunters were not happy to hear they had to leave. For some strange reason, they felt they had a right to be there, private property or not.

When they gave her a hard time, Jamie said, "Would you like it if we went hunting in *your* yard?"

They left.

It was the first time the Stemples heard, "We've been coming out here for years . . ." and unfortunately, it wouldn't be the last.

The three traipsed back to the home site, and Jamie hoped nobody noticed how bad she was shaking. Luke returned with straighter boards, and the four knuckled down to framing the floor and exterior walls.

On Monday morning, Jamie grabbed the phone on her way out the door.

"Hi, Jamie, this is Evelyn from Dr. Branson's office. He'd like you to come in as soon as possible."

Jamie thought for a second. "Okay . . . how about Wednesday morning?"

"How about today at three?"

"Well, did he say why?"

"You'll have to discuss that with him. Three o'clock then?"

It was pointless to argue with Evelyn. "Fine . . . I'll be there." She hung up the phone, and sat down in the nearest chair. *I can't afford two office visits.*

Her thoughts turned to the day she met Sam Andrews. *It's time for some answers.* She hunted for his phone number, and then dialed.

"Sam speaking."

"Sam—hi, it's Jamie Stemple."

There was a pause before he said anything.

"Jamie . . . are you okay?"

"I'm fine—and what do you mean by that? In fact, what did you mean by all those things you said to me?"

Another pause.

"Uh . . . have you seen a doctor?"

"I had a physical last week, but they won't give me the results over the phone. You'd think it was top secret or something—or is it because they won't get paid if I don't walk into the office—"

"Jamie!"

"Sorry, I was on a roll. This is all driving me crazy! But I don't know why I'm telling you this, I hardly know you—which brings me to my next point—"

"Jamie . . . I have to go now—but know that I'm here for you, and we'll talk soon." With that he hung up.

Jamie was left with a dial tone, and one more unanswered question. *What did that mean?*

She planned to swing by the library after her appointment; but her research on the town doomed by Mormon crickets, would have to wait. She had other things on her mind. For instance, how was she going to pay for another series of tests, when she couldn't pay for the first ones? And why did they need more tests anyways? It was only a headache.

By the time Jamie got back home, Evelyn had made her an appointment for Wednesday, in Wenatchee.

"Jamie, they need you there by eight-thirty to fill out paperwork. Do you need directions?"

"I need answers."

"That's the reason for the appointment."

If she'd had a sense of humor, Evelyn would have been the perfect nurse. But to her credit, she was efficient, and always had the correct brush-off for those questions she wasn't allowed to answer.

Jamie didn't know what to tell Luke, so she decided to tell him nothing. He had too much on his mind already.

Wednesday came and went. And again she was waiting for results. Waiting . . . now there's something that had become commonplace. But then, anything does, given time.

On Friday morning, Jamie putted around the house, preparing for Luke's fifty-ninth homecoming. When the phone rang, it was Evelyn.

"Jamie, Dr. Branson has your test results, and would like you to come in at noon if possible."

"Today?"

"Yes, please."

"Well, why don't you have him call me, then he won't miss his lunch time."

"He won't, he's taking a late lunch."

"Evelyn . . . the truth is, I can't afford another office visit."

"I'm sorry, Jamie, but he needs to see you. So, can I tell him noon?"

Jamie agreed and hung up. *That's putting your foot down, Jamie.*

That afternoon, the clouds turned dark. So did Jamie's heart. She sped on the highway, not caring what the speed limit was. Rain hit the windshield the same time tears hit her cheek. She turned left on the gravel road, and for the first time, was oblivious to the beauty around her. She pulled in the gate, drove up the driveway, then on into the sagebrush. She got out of the car, left the door hanging open, and started up the steep embankment on the backside of her mesa.

The higher she climbed, the louder she cried. The lichen-covered rocks were wet and slick. She slipped twice, scraping her hands and bruising her legs. She reached the top, screamed out in agony, and dropped to her knees. Slapping her hand on the rocks, she screamed:

"WHERE ARE YOU? IS THIS THE BREAKTHROUGH YOU PROMISED? I TRUSTED YOU!"

She covered her face with both hands. "What have I done? I've made a mess of everything—and there's no time to fix it!"

The answer was immediate. "I am here. Take My hand."

Jamie kept her face covered. "No! I don't want to die!"

Chapter Ten

"Uh . . . Mom? Mom!"

"*What?*" Kayla shouted, and wiped tears off her cheek.

"I think you'd better pull over."

"Why?" Then Kayla glanced in the mirror. "Oh . . . great."

There wasn't much of a shoulder, so she pulled off the best she could, and dug for her wallet.

Riley frowned. "I don't know, Mom, he looks kind of mean."

"Great."

The officer leaned down to the window. "Good afternoon, may I see your license, registration, and proof of insurance, please?"

Kayla handed them over, and he studied each piece. After a pause, he said, "Are you okay, Miss?"

"I'm fine."

"From Seattle, huh?"

"Uh . . . yes."

He walked to the patrol car, and then returned a few minutes later. He handed back her information, and smoothed his silver mustache with two fingers.

"Do you know what the speed limit is on this road?"

"No . . . I'm afraid I don't," Kayla said.

"And do you know how fast you were going?"

"No . . . I'm afraid I don't know that either."

"Well . . . the speed limit is fifty-five, and you were going seventy-one."

"I'm sorry, I—"

Riley piped up. "It's my fault, sir. She was telling me this story and—"

"—You got so involved that you didn't realize how fast you were driving, and you didn't see the posted limit—I know, I've heard it all before." He paused and drew in a deep breath. "Okay—I'm going to let you off this time—IF, you promise me you'll slow down—and pay attention."

"I will. I promise."

"And you're sure you're okay?"

Kayla nodded.

"All right. Have a nice day." He adjusted his hat, and turned to walk away. "Oh . . ." he said, turning back around, ". . . nice car."

"Thank you," Kayla said with her head out the window.

"Go, Mom—before he changes his mind."

Kayla got back on the road . . . nice and legal like. "That was too close. What's wrong with me?"

For twenty miles, on the straightest road they'd ever driven, they passed acres of sweet corn, grain corn, alfalfa, onions, sugar beets, potatoes and wheat; appropriately marked with little blue and white signs.

Kayla pointed at Riley's side window. "Look at the dust devil!"

"Cool!" Riley said, as they watched the twisting column of dust twirl across the field. "What causes them?"

"Uh . . . let's see . . . if I remember this right, they're formed by hot air rising from hot spots in the ground. And when the air rises rapidly—like in a chimney—it creates a vortex that pulls cooler air and debris up with it."

"Hmm, that's pretty good for a sworn city girl."

"What?"

You know what I mean, Mom. We could've lived over here. Grandpa would've loved it."

Kayla sunk down a bit, and stared at the road ahead. As they passed the "Welcome to Breezley" sign, Riley broke another silence.

"When I was doing my senior project, I learned a lot about the small towns in this Columbia Basin area. Did you know that Breezley, Annie Lake, and Adalon aren't the original town names?

"Uh, huh . . ." Kayla mumbled, without breaking her focus. "I need to make a stop." She turned into the Safeway lot, and parked a safe distance from the cart return area.

"So . . . is this the store Grandma Jamie shopped at?"

Kayla stared at the store. "Yeah, but back then it was further down the street, where the furniture store is. And it was a lot smaller." Without realizing it, Kayla pulled the silver locket out from inside her T-shirt, and held onto it.

"Riley, would you run in for me?"

"Sure—what do you need?"

"A bag of frozen lima beans . . . and get something to drink if you want."

"Ha! You did forget. Wait till I tell Grandpa!

"You better not."

Riley jumped out and disappeared behind the automatic door. Kayla leaned back and stared at the sky. A breeze played with feathered cirrus clouds, and her mind played with memories . . . so much so, that she didn't see the two men walk in front of her car. And when Riley opened the door, she jumped.

"Mom, did you see those two guys in front of me?"

"No . . . why?"

"I don't know. They kept staring at me—like they knew me."

"It's because you're cute."

"No, Mom! Not like that, they were old. One was about your age, and the other had to be as old as Grandpa."

"Well, maybe you remind them of someone."

"Hmm . . . maybe . . . I don't know—they looked Indian or something, and the younger one was wearing—oh never mind—here are your beans."

"Thanks, Honey," Kayla said, and started the car.

A mom and her teenage kids crossed in front of them. The girl was riding on the shopping cart, the boy was pushing it, and the mom was tickling him in the ribs. Kayla rubbed the locket again, and her eyes glossed over.

"That looks like Grandma, Chris, and I, twenty years ago."

"Mom . . . I understand now, why this story's so hard for you . . . it would be for me too. So, it's okay if you don't want to finish it."

Kayla looked out her side window. *Oddly enough, it was getting easier.* "No . . . I need to finish it."

They drove through downtown, and stopped for a red light. Kayla glanced up at the clock on the right side of the intersection. It was two-thirty.

"Hey! Remember the movie, *Always?* Did you know a lot of it was filmed here?"

Shocked by the outburst, Riley took a moment to respond. "Where?"

"I'll show you," Kayla said, and clicked on her turn indicator. When the light turned green, she made a right turn, crossed over the railroad tracks and headed up the hill. They drove past residential streets, a tiny market, churches, and two schools. The road veered to the right, and then straight ahead was the Port of Breezley, and the municipal airport.

Kayla pointed to the older hanger. "There it is! Flat Rock Air Attack Training Base."

"Really?" Riley leaned forward to get a good look. "Cool!"

"Yep, welcome to Flat Rock, Colorado!"

"So, you were here for that, Mom?"

"No, it was the late eighties . . . you were about seven."

"Oh . . . but you knew about it at the time?"

"Oh yeah. A classmate of mine lives up here somewhere, and she made a point to call me. She was strolling with her three-year-old and a few neighbors, when the film crew returned from shooting a scene—remember the one where John Goodman is doused with fire retardant?"

Kayla pulled into the parking lot and stopped the car.

"Then what?" Riley asked, as Kayla stared at the runway.

"Apparently, the little boy waved at dozens of cars, but nobody waved back. Finally, a guy at the tail end, on a four-wheeler, smiled and waved at him. It was Steven Spielberg. Needless to say, they were elated, and snuck behind the barricade for a closer look. Spielberg spotted them; but instead of making them leave, he posed in a picture with them."

"That's cool. So, were you jealous?"

"Of course—we're talking Steven Spielberg here! But that's why she called me. Back then, everyone knew what I wanted to be.

A maintenance truck cruised by, and the driver eyed their Camaro.

"I have an idea. Let's go the long way past Annie Lake and up through Adalon."

"Are you sure, Mom? Don't you think Grandpa's getting worried about us?"

No . . . I've got a feeling Grandpa knows exactly what's going on. And besides, we're getting close to the ranch, and there's still so much to tell you."

They backtracked to the main road, and headed east on a six-mile stretch that separated the two towns. It was the perfect time of day to catch the effect of sunlight falling on sprinkler mist. The colors were beautiful: red, orange, yellow, green, indigo, and violet. And for Kayla, they brought back another piece of the story.

At the interchange, they turned left and drove through Annie Lake. Most of the business district was on the left side of the highway; and a peek down Main Street gave the flavor of an old Wild West town.

"You know, Riley, done right, Annie Lake would be the perfect resort town."

They drove past the city park and pink motel, and then accelerated to forty-five and headed out of town.

"So, my studious daughter . . . in all your research, did you discover why this town was renamed "Annie Lake?"

"Yeah, I did. It was named after an eccentric lady who lived here in the early 1900s. Her name was Anna Mae, but everyone called her 'Sagebrush Annie.'"

"I guess you did do your homework. Did you also know that she lived alone out here in a rundown cabin, never owned a car—got around by hitchhiking, wrote a great poem, and was one of the first entrepreneurs around to promote recreation as a business?

"Wow, Mom . . . how is it that you know so much about her?"

"Grandma's research."

Riley waited to hear what Kayla would say next.

"Grandma read me her poem; but all I can remember is something about 'a pinto horse with wings.' Why is it, we forget so many good things when faced with something bad?"

"I don't know, Mom."

"Adalon—twenty-two miles." Kayla looked across Annie Lake, and took a deep breath. "It won't be long now."

They drove in silence; both of them entranced with the stark beauty of the tall coulee walls. And for Kayla, the brewing continued.

After a few miles, Riley crinkled her face. "Is it raining?"

"Huh?"

"It sounds like rain."

Kayla studied the windshield. "It is—bugs."

"Gross!" Riley said, as a yellow 'splat' hit the glass.

"Bugs and rain . . . ." Kayla paused, "I never did like the rain."

"Uh, Mom, then why do we live in Seattle?"

Chapter Eleven

It was raining, it was late, and somehow, it was May 25, 1978. Ten days past their deadline.

Jamie yanked the paper from the electronic typewriter, threw it across the room, and burst into tears. Rock was at his usual spot under the desk, and put his head in her lap.

"I can't do this anymore!" she cried out, and pushed all her notes on the floor. "I quit!"

She stomped to the kitchen, shook open a black garbage bag, and proceeded to throw in all the pages, her notes, her folders chalked full of research, her reference books, rejection letters, stories in different stages; and in a final fit, grabbed her journal from under the sofa, and tossed it in too.

Kayla came out, rubbing her eyes. "Mom?"

"—Huh? Sorry, did I wake you?"

"Are you all right, Mom?"

"I'm fine—go back to bed."

She carried the bulging bag past Kayla and out to the garbage can. Upon her return, she unplugged the typewriter, wound up the cord, and put on the gray plastic cover. If it had fit, it would've been in the can, too.

Kayla shook her head and went back to bed. Jamie threw her blankets on the sofa, and plunked down on top of them. The glow from the cross seemed twice as bright, and was the last thing she wanted to look at. She jumped up to close the blinds, and in her haste, made enough noise with the metal, that she woke both Rock and the dog next door.

How did life get so bad?

Finally, sleep took over, and Jamie dreamt of Teri again.

Same as before: Jamie was standing in an open place, behind the girl with long blond hair. A man yelled, "Teri!" and she started to turn around. At the point where Jamie usually woke up, she didn't.

The girl slowly turned and looked right at Jamie, who gasped, and jerked herself awake.

Once again, it was two o'clock in the morning, and her heart thumped clear to her toes. Out of habit, she reached for her journal; and then remembered where it was.

At seven-thirty, the kids left for school; and two hours later, when the phone rang, she was still sitting on the couch.

"Hello?"

"Hi, Jamie, it's Sam . . . I've been worried about you."

"Well don't be—I'm fine."

"It's okay to tell your kids that; but it doesn't work with me. So, what are you doing today?"

"Why?" Jamie asked, looking at the bare desk.

"I'm coming to see you. It will take me about an hour, so . . . how's eleven o'clock?"

"Sam, I don't have time. Luke's coming home tonight, and I have a lot to do."

"Have you told him yet?"

"No! And stay out of it—it's none of your business." She closed her eyes, and gripped the phone.

"Too late for that, Jamie . . . so I'll meet you at your property at eleven?"

"No! I can't go out there."

"Okay, in town then."

"No! My neighbor watches me like a hawk. That's all Luke and I don't need right now."

"Okay, miss 'No,' it's settled. Your property at eleven o'clock—or I give your neighbor a scenario to chew on." Click.

Jamie hung up the phone and grumbled all the way to the shower.

Like the day they met, she was late, and speeding on Hawkins Road. And just like before, as she rounded the last corner, the tall Indian man was there, waiting patiently at the gate.

"Isn't spring beautiful?"

Jamie looked around. "I hadn't noticed."

"Yeah—right! You're the one who can spot a bird on top of the coulee wall."

"So."

They pulled open the gate, and drove up to the house. Jamie hesitated before getting out of her car; not Sam, he was already out, walking around, checking out the house.

"Wow! This place looks great."

"Yeah . . . ."

Sam trekked to the back of the house. "I love all the windows. You must have a view from every room."

"Yeah . . . every room."

"I noticed the realtor sign."

"Who hasn't," Jamie said and kicked a rock near her foot.

"So, how are you doing?" He said in a serious tone.

"We still have the laminate, floor coverings, and trim work to do."

"It looks great, but actually, I was referring to your health."

"Oh. Well new topic then."

Sam shook his head. "Okay. Where's your flute? I haven't heard it in a long time."

Jamie mumbled, "And I thought *I* asked a lot of questions."

"Well?"

"It doesn't matter, Sam! And I'm the one who should be getting answers here. I've known you for what—eight months now—and you still haven't explained how you hear my flute, knew about that snake—and knew I had a brain tumor, when I didn't even know!"

Jamie kicked at the ground, and raised her voice even more. "So, of course, you already know it's inoperable."

He gave her time to be angry, then said, "I think you're a very brave woman. I wish we had met a hundred years ago. You would've looked great in regalia."

"Thanks, Sam." She said, and slumped her shoulders. "But I'm not brave. If I had known what was going to happen, I would've stayed in Seattle."

"No you wouldn't. You have courage . . . and a listening heart."

"No . . . actually, I just want to find the edge of the world, and jump off. But with my luck, I'd probably land on something soft."

Sam crossed his arms and studied her face.

Jamie frowned. "What's that, your stoic Indian look?"

He took a step backwards and braced himself. Without looking at her eyes, he said, "Okay . . . we'll trade information. You tell me where your flute is, and I'll tell you how I knew those things."

"Fine . . . I pawned it . . . along with my heirloom jewelry. I had to. I had doctor bills and no money. There! Your turn."

"What do you mean—you *had* doctor bills?"

"Sam, I'm not going to waste time and money going to the doctor when there's nothing they can do."

"Okay," he said, looking down the coulee, "walk with me."

He grabbed her hand, and headed through the sage. "Have you seen the bobcat, yet? He has a den up in those rocks."

"How do you . . . ? Never mind."

Sam smiled and pointed out the red-tailed hawk, swallows rebuilding their homes, the camas root, coyote and mule deer tracks, and the smell of spring sage. He launched into the medicinal properties of sage, why their leaves are coated with hairs, and why they change throughout the year; but Jamie interrupted.

"Sam, come on, we had a deal."

He stopped short, and sat down on a large boulder. After motioning for her to sit beside him, he folded his hands together, was quiet for a moment, and then began.

"The Creator puts gifts in our hearts; and we must decide if we use them or not. If we're wise, we do. But, there's a price . . . and I think you've already learned this."

Jamie managed a half smile, and looked down the coulee. *The sage does smell good today.*

"Knowing things is one of my gifts." He looked down at his hands and continued in a low voice. "And to you, I gave a portion of my heart . . . and that hurts."

It was Jamie's turn to cross her arms. "Why? I was a total stranger when we met. That couldn't have hurt too much to know that I—"

Sam put his folded hands up to his chin. "That you're dying . . . ? You're wrong. It hurts very much."

"Why?"

He closed his eyes and didn't move or speak. Jamie didn't know what to think, so she didn't move either. Rock was the only one who appeared alive, as he zigzagged through sage following the scent of unseen critters.

After what seemed like forever, Sam stood up and pulled his wallet from a back pocket. He opened it, and pulled out a picture of a white woman, that had been tucked in behind Shep's school picture. He smoothed the corner, and handed it to Jamie.

Jamie never posed for this picture—but it could have been her at age twenty-five.

Sam crossed his arms tight across his chest, and cleared his throat. "She disappeared in 1961 . . . she is my wife."

For a moment, there were no sounds. As if all paused to pay respect to hearts that were hurting. Even Rock was still.

"Sam . . . I don't know what to say . . . I am so sorry."

"You even talk like her. That first time on the phone you scared me to death. And then when I saw you, especially your eyes, a spear pierced my heart . . . and I was hoping—"

"Sam . . . I'm not her."

"I know," he whispered.

"What happened to her?"

"I don't know. She flew to Seattle to see her aunt . . . and never came home. I moved out here so I could find her."

He looked away. And she understood why.

"I'm so sorry, Sam . . . what was her name?"

He looked down at the picture cupped in her hands. "You already know."

Energy pulsed through her veins, and she stood up. With a dry throat, she said, "Her name is 'Teri,' isn't it?"

As hard as it was for Sam, he smiled. "You've been given a gift, Jamie . . . an opportunity to be part of something big planned by The Creator; a plan that will touch your family for generations to come."

He paused a moment. "But, it all hinges on what you do right now, while there's still time. And you have to figure it out. What does it mean . . . to be Jamie Stemple? What has The Creator put in your heart?"

"But—"

"Shhhh." Sam said like a teacher, with his index finger up to his mouth. He got up and started back to the house. Her answer would come. And he knew he was not the one she needed to talk to.

Jamie sat back down, and her brain tried to absorb what just took place.

Sam waited for her; and in leaving, said, "Pray every day. And no matter what, always give thanks for what He's given you. For the day will come, when you won't have to search for things to be thankful for."

Tears poured from her eyes, and she dropped her head on Sam's chest. He closed his eyes, and put his hand on her head, over the spot where the tumor was. It was one of those rare moments, between true friends.

As Sam drove away, Jamie sat on the front step of the new home. She leaned on one elbow, and put her other arm around Rock. Together they stared at the mesa, and Jamie thought out loud.

"Luke was right; it really does look like a giant Aussie hat. Luke . . . I wish I could tell you everything."

Upon leaving, she stopped to close the gate, and in a quick decision, yanked out the realtor's sign and threw it in the trunk.

"We're not selling our home!" she yelled, for Rock and all the wildlife to hear.

Back in Adalon, Chris was at the court shooting hoops.

"Hi, Chris!" said a tall man with blond hair.

Chris wheeled around to see who'd caught him skipping class.

"Uh . . . hi . . . how'd you know my name?"

"I've seen you around. I'm Mark—care for a game of pig?"

"Sure!" Chris smirked, since he had to be thirty-some years old.

"Great!" Mark said, and rolled up the sleeves of his white shirt. "This must be a holiday?"

"Huh? I don't think so—why?"

"You're not in school, I assumed it was."

"Oh . . ." Chris nodded his head.

After thirty minutes of play, they sat down to rest.

"Okay, Chris, here's the deal. I get one chance to make a half-court shot, from the left corner—and if I make it, you have to stay in school.

"Ha! What's the point of that—nobody makes it from there—not with one shot." Chris stood up and dribbled in place.

"Well, do we have a deal or not?"

"Sure—won't bother me."

Mark snatched the ball away, and walked back to the half-court line. He sized up the distance, dribbled the ball twice, and threw it. It never touched the rim.

Chris' mouth dropped wide open.

"Well, now!" Mark said, throwing the ball at Chris. "That's kind of interesting." He unrolled his sleeves, buttoned the cuffs, and turned to leave. "Hey, do you work at your property on weekends?"

"Yeah . . . *why?*"

Mark waved. "Good—there's someone you need to meet. See you in school!"

Chris walked out to the half court line, stared at the hoop, and tried to figure out what just happened.

Jamie was on Main Street, and would have seen Chris at the court, if her thoughts hadn't been locked on Teri. *A piece fit into place . . . but what was the place?* She pulled up to her house, and almost ran into the garbage can.

It was garbage pick-up day, and for the first time in months, Chris had put out the can without a reminder.

She walked through the gate, up to the porch, and it wasn't until she was inside, and set her purse on the desk, that it hit her. The garbage can. Garbage day! She

124

ran outside, opened the lid, and felt sick. *Now what have I done?*

The phone was ringing as she walked back in the house. She hesitated, and grabbed it on the fourth ring. It was the principal—again. Chris had skipped school—again. And this was his last chance—again. Jamie thanked him for his call, and said she would handle it. Again.

She hung up, and took a deep breath.

That night, the aroma of garlic, basil, and oregano filled the little house. Angel hair pasta simmered on the stove, a green salad chilled, and a loaf of sourdough waited by the oven. Jamie pulled the table out, set it for four, placed two candles in the middle, and retrieved two chairs from the garage. After checking her work, she swept the porch and straightened the welcome mat. Then she checked her work a second time, just to be sure.

Kayla came through the house, plunked her books down on the desk, and headed for the bedroom. "Hi, Mom, how are ya doing?"

For a split second, Jamie hesitated. "I'm fine—how was your day?"

"Good. We're reading *Roots*—it was made into a TV movie, you know."

Jamie smiled and glanced down at the books. She picked up the math book with her right hand, *Roots* with her left, and while holding both books, thought her eyes were going bad.

First, there was a flash of white. And then the two books blurred together into one. And no matter how many times she blinked, she only saw one—she could feel two—but only saw one opened book. The pages were flipping, but they were blank. Then a second book appeared. And like transparencies placed on an overhead projector, the written pages from the second book were being placed into the first book. She couldn't make out the words, but could feel the weight of the books shift as the pages transferred over. Then both books closed. One had a worn, soft black cover, and the other wore a title, blurred at first, but slowly, it became clear . . . *Place . . . of . . . Sage.*

Just then, a truck pulled up. It was Luke. He was early. Jamie looked at the two books in her hands, *Principles in Mathematics* and *Roots,* blinked a few more times, and set them back on the desk. She braced herself, and shifted mentally, before going out to greet him.

She was glad he was home; but it was hard to see him. The circles under his eyes were dark, and silver streaks were in his hair.

After dinner, they cleared the table, and he asked the dreaded question. "Do you have any news for me, James?"

"Uh . . . not yet," she answered, without looking up.

"Then I'm assuming the *For Sale* sign is in your trunk?"

She nodded.

On Saturday morning, a thunderstorm was in the works. Luke and Chris left early to buy materials, while Jamie and Kayla put together lunch.

Two hours later, the girls arrived at the property, and dark nimbus clouds rolled in. They pulled up to the house as Luke threw a hammer out the door.

"Great . . . there goes another one," Jamie mumbled as they slowly got out of the car.

Kayla examined the broken hammer, and Jamie made her way in the house. Luke was on his hands and knees, pounding down nail heads, and scraping off sheet rock mud.

"Hi!" Jamie said, setting the food on a sawhorse table.

He didn't answer. But that was okay, she understood.

"I have to run into town later, do you want me to buy a new hammer?"

"With *what*?" he snapped.

"What's wrong, Luke?"

"*WHAT'S WRONG?* What do you think? It's bad enough that we're losing everything, but do you have to rub my face in it?"

"*What?* What are you talking about?"

"Care to guess who I ran into at the lumber store?"

Jamie knew that phone call would come back to haunt her. She tried to think of what to say, but couldn't get her mouth to form words.

Luke pounded the hammer into the floor. "Did you think I wouldn't find out? The inn offered you a job—a

127

good one! How could you say no? Don't you realize what's at stake here?"

Outside, the thunder moved closer, and black clouds hovered overhead.

"You had no intention of getting a job, did you? You've lied to me for two years; adding just enough to string me along, keep me working—"

Kayla and Chris burst through the door.

"—Then you'd throw in a few words about God to make it sound real convincing!"

Thunder shook the new windows; and lightning flashed above the coulee wall. Chris and Kayla grabbed a pop and backed themselves out the door. It was safer outside with the lightning.

Wind howled through the canyon, and then came rain as loud as hail—so much, so fast, that it created waterfalls from the top of the wall, and etched out small streams down the dirt driveway.

Later that night, when the kids were asleep, Jamie heard Luke break down in the shower. His agony dropped her to her knees, as she pictured him leaning against the wet wall, hot water pounding on his body and mingling with tears. Jamie covered her face, and whispered, "Please, Father, let it be over soon."

Then He spoke. "Write it now, while the pain is real."

A waterline burst from her soul. "But I threw it all away!"

The next morning, Luke was out of the house by six. Jamie, Chris, and Kayla packed up lunch and snacks, and were at the property by eight.

When they pulled up, Luke was carrying two saw-horses, two extension cords, and a toolbox down the stairs. They had to clear out everything; carpet was coming first thing Monday morning.

It was a day of few words. And even fewer smiles.

That evening, Luke packed his duffle bag, and headed back over the mountain. Jamie sat down on the sofa, and stared at nothing. *Please, Father, keep him safe for me.*

Kayla opened her bedroom door, and the lyrics of Jim Croce's "Time In a Bottle" made Jamie's heart ache.

"Mom?"

Jamie looked up, and there was Kayla standing in front of her.

"I need to talk to you."

"Okay, but only if it's good . . . I don't think I can handle much more." Jamie looked at Kayla's concerned face, and pulled her down next to her. "So what's up?"

"I have something to give you. And this might sound a little strange—but then, with you maybe not . . . anyways, here it goes. I have something that belongs to you, and I was sitting on my bed listening to music, and I heard this voice say, 'The time has come,' and . . . oh—just a minute."

Kayla darted into the bedroom, and returned a moment later. "What were you thinking? Here, I believe this belongs to you." She plopped the bulging black garbage bag in Jamie's lap. "I couldn't let you do it."

"Mom! You have heard His voice! You said it yourself, 'The time has come . . .'"

"Riley, this isn't *The Princess Bride* I'm telling here—so quit interrupting."

"But, Mom, don't you see? You did the same thing to Grandma Jamie, that I did to you when you tried to sell your filmmaking books."

"I mean it, Riley. Just let me finish."

"As you wish."

"Very funny . . . ."

"Whatever, Mom . . . but you know I'm right."

Chapter Twelve

There they were . . . all the ingredients . . . dropped in her lap . . . .

An hour passed. Jamie still didn't move.

"Goodnight, Mom," Chris and Kayla said, coming around the corner. But when Jamie didn't see or hear them, they shrugged their shoulders and went to bed.

Unbeknownst to Jamie, the sun was setting; the town hums softened, crickets prepared for a concert, and across her land, the rose hue changed to purple.

Without looking, she reached in the bag, and pulled out her journal. For a moment, she held it close like a new mother holds a baby; but then she choked on the lump in her throat, and threw the journal across the room.

"I don't want to die!" she said aloud, but not loud enough for the kids to hear. She covered her face with a pillow and cried, "I'm only thirty-six!"

Her journal landed face up, with the front cover bent backwards underneath the TV stand. She stared at it until she couldn't stand it any longer, and walked over to pick it up. As she bent down, the scent of sage overpowered the room, and her hands began to shake. She sat on the carpet and waited for the seizure to pass. They were happening more frequently now. When it ended, Jamie grabbed the journal and read page one that it was opened to.

May 17, 1976:

God said, "This is the way . . . walk in it." And I have a feeling life will never be the same again.

Her tears dripped on the page. "Why? I did what you said."

The next morning—even before coffee—Luke called. Jamie winced at the sound of his voice, as he reminded her they had defaulted on their loan, and foreclosure proceedings would begin in sixty days. What could she say?

Father, please help us . . . we can't handle much more.

Later that morning, the phone rang again; and as much as she didn't want to pick it up, she did.

"Hello?"

"Hi, Jamie!"

"Sam . . . what are you doing?"

"Calling you. Do you have time for a friend?"

"Sam—I . . ."

"I know—you don't feel so good. But I want to show you something. Can you meet me somewhere?"

"No, not at the property—I can't."

"Actually, I want you to meet me up at the dam."

"Grand Coulee? Why?"

"You'll see. Just meet me at noon, at the top of the dam. I'll be the one posing with Mr. Roosevelt."

"I don't know, Sam, I—"

Click.

"Sam? Oh, Great!"

Jamie hung up the phone, and looked at the clock. "Ten-thirty—this is ridiculous!"

Rock lifted his head to show concern.

"There's not enough gas to last a week, and he expects me to drive seventy miles in one day!"

Forty-five minutes later, she jotted a quick note to the kids, and bent down to explain to Rock why he couldn't go with her. He followed her out to the porch, then plunked himself down, and put his head between his paws.

The day was shaping up to be classic spring. Early morning winds cleared out the clouds, so Jamie drove north under a blue sky, with the sun-kissed water of Banks Lake—the equalizing reservoir—on her left.

Boy, if we had been here for my ninth birthday, we could've seen the Grand Coulee without water. I wonder how the people felt, giving up their homes for progress.

Numerous cars, trucks, and recreational vehicles were parked in turnout areas along the lake. Folks were fishing, snapping pictures, having picnics, bird watching, walking their pets, and switching drivers.

Jamie thought of a story she had read in an old issue of the *Adalon News*. It noted that, as the pumps at Grand Coulee Dam filled the coulee with water, the town of Adalon had to guard against a rattlesnake invasion. Nightly patrols were sent out to kill snakes before they got to town; and in one fifteen-minute period, one hundred rattlers had been killed near Steamboat Rock. *Poor snakes.*

Jamie accelerated up the incline of the "Million Dollar Mile," which was actually a two-mile cut through the coulee wall. From what she read, the expensive cut had to be made because the foundation material along the bottom of the wall was too soft for a roadbed. But in doing so, it opened up a view that could not have been matched from below.

As Jamie approached the crest of the hill, and prepared herself for the view, a strange thing happened. She passed through a section that was like a tunnel with no top, and saw a white flash—

—And suddenly it was 1955. She was thirteen years old, wearing a plaid print dress, with a skinny little belt; sitting in the back seat of their brand new '55 two-tone green and tan Chevrolet Belair; her dad's pride and joy.

From where she sat, she could see her dad in the mirror. He wore a starched white shirt; and that gray and black Fedora hat he wore on outings, covered his dark hair. And her mom, well she always looked like a million. This day she was wearing her light blue, three-quarter-sleeve cardigan with covered buttons, and woven tweed skirt to match. The color was perfect with her blond hair.

"So, Jamie," her dad said, looking in the mirror, "What do you want to be when you grow up?"

Jamie was quiet a moment, and then answered, "A writer."

"Great! And what are you going to write?"

Jamie looked out the window in awe as the canyon opened up. "An important book . . . maybe about a place like this."

"And I bet you will, Honey," her mom said; and her parents looked at each other and smiled—

—In a white flash, Jamie saw the car coming up fast, and realized she was only going thirty-four m.p.h. She pulled over and took a deep breath as the muscle car zoomed by.

Twenty-six miles into the trip, she was still driving along Banks Lake. The terrain had changed a bit, though. Pale brown rocks were added to the palette, and pine trees appeared to be springing from them. The overall scene was like a pastel painting brushed with watercolors.

Jamie drove through the historic towns of Electric City and Grand Coulee, and headed down to the dam.

Sam, on time of course, was exactly where he said he'd be—posed on the railing by the bust of our thirty-second president, a key figure in the Grand Coulee Dam project.

"Hey—no hat today!"

"Yeah . . . hi, Sam."

Sam gave her one of his hugs, and stood back to look at her. "Check it out—we match!"

Sure enough, they were both in blue jeans, white T-shirts and boots. Jamie couldn't help but smile.

"I like that smile," Sam said, and headed for her car.

Jamie looked around the parking lot. "Sam, how did you get here?"

"A friend. I left my 'bug' at his house."

"Now there's a site, you crammed into a Volkswagen Beetle."

"Hey now! I like my car."

"Okay, fine. So what are we doing up here? Touring the dam?"

"Nope. Let's go, and you'll find out."

Jamie stared at the massive concrete structure. "Sam . . . what do you think of the dam?"

"I think that's another story; and right now I want to talk about you."

Jamie frowned. "Well I don't."

Sam crossed his arms, and set his jaw.

"Oh, great. There's that stoic Indian look again."

"Jamie, you have to tell him."

"Sam—you don't understand! This is the man I've loved since I was fifteen . . . he's my best friend, and he thinks I've betrayed him. And that's exactly what it looks like! He's been stripped of every comfort trying to get us settled here—And now, after everything I've put him through, I'm supposed to look in his eyes and say, 'Oh, Honey, by the way, did I mention I'm dying?' How can I do that to him?"

Sam was silent as they weaved down through Coulee Dam, and onto the bridge that separates the east part of town from the west. From the middle of the bridge, they captured the full effect of progress: the gigantic dam on one side, and remains of the mighty Columbia River on the other.

Jamie felt bad about her outburst, and looked at Sam. "So my wise friend . . . do you know your dam stats?"

"My 'dam stats?' You mean like, this concrete giant is 5,223 ft. long . . . only 57 feet short of a mile, as tall as the Washington Memorial . . . 550 ft. high, and generates more power than a million locomotives?"

"Smart alec—so you've read the brochure . . . but a million locomotives?"

"He has to know, Jamie."

"Sam—do you want out right here?"

"Uh, no thank you—we're almost there!"

"Good." Jamie said, shaking her head.

"You know, if I didn't care, I wouldn't say anything."

"Sam!"

Sam crossed his arms, and then remembered he was in charge of directions. "Left—take a left!"

Jamie hit the brakes, and made a quick turn. Luckily, no one was tailgating—they would've been in her trunk.

"Oh, by the way . . . happy birthday!"

Jamie rolled her eyes. "It's not my birthday, yet . . . and I'm not celebrating anyways."

"Well I am! Another year's beginning for you."

"Yeah . . . but will I see it end?"

"There's only One who knows that answer."

"Yeah . . . and He's keeping quiet."

"Are you sure? He speaks to you in a lot of different ways."

"I know . . . let's drop it, okay, Sam? So where are we headed?"

"At the end of this block, hang a right, and it'll be the last building on the right."

"Who lives here?" Jamie asked as she pulled up to the curb in front of a small yellow, box-like house.

"Someone who wants to talk to you."

"*To me?* Why?"

"He wants to meet the skinny white woman he sees out on the mound."

"The mound?" Jamie asked, careful to not trip on the cracked sidewalk.

"Your mesa," Sam answered, and knocked once on the short front door before ducking a bit, and going in. He must have heard a "come in," but Jamie didn't. She hesitated, but then walked in quickly to stay close to Sam, and almost ran into him.

"Stay here," Sam said, and left the living room before she could argue.

The inside looked like a tribal museum: baskets, pictures, books on Chief Joseph, a root digging stick propped up in the corner, a bowl for burning sage. She walked over to four baskets, all woven with geometrical designs and grouped together. She was so absorbed she didn't see the man with gray braids sitting in the corner recliner, and when he cleared his throat, she jumped.

He laughed, and then said, "The baskets belonged to my grandmother; and her grandmother before her. They've been handed down for six generations. And through those baskets we have kept their memories alive. And to answer your next question: there weren't any granddaughters in my family—only grandsons. And you're wondering why you're here, so sit with me. Have some tea."

Jamie smiled. After being around Sam, she was getting use to answers to silent questions.

"What kind is it?" she asked pulling up a wooden chair, "sage?"

"Lipton," he said, and grinned.

Jamie started to laugh. And then something inside broke loose. Suddenly, tears were rolling down her face. She wondered where Sam was, and why she was a blubbering idiot in front of this man she had not been formally introduced to.

"Well—I'd like to know the name of the person I'm making a fool of myself for."

"I'm Ben," the Nez Perce elder said, and reached out for her hand. "And you're not making a fool of yourself. Your heart is revealing itself."

Jamie put her hand in his. He closed it tight and closed his eyes. After a long silence, broken only by Jamie trying not to cry, he began.

"People today walk the wide road, it's easier; you can stumble and not be noticed. But when you walk the narrow road, the way is rough, and to stumble means to stop those behind you. And sometimes, it takes a person to come up behind us, and help us stand back up. That's what Sam is to you—that is why the Creator put him in your life, along with the elder woman who makes bread. They help stand you up when you fall."

He paused, giving her time to think on what he said, and then he continued.

"You have a good heart. Your land tells me so. The water tells of your pain, your joy. When your heart soars, it is blue as the sky; but on your dark days, it is black as night. Pay attention to the water. In a place that appears desolate, the water gives it life. But not just any water. For you, it's like the heart that beats in your chest. Why do you think that is? Go to the water and listen."

Jamie felt someone enter the room, and looked up to see Sam.

Ben's expression was serious as he said to her, "Jamie, you are young. But your situation has made you an elder. Think about this, and base your decisions on this knowledge."

He slowly stood up, and walked over to the bowl of burnt sage. He rubbed a small amount between his thumb and index finger, and then smudged Jamie's forehead.

"The Creator speaks to your heart. Listen for Him. He will guide you, and give you peace."

"Thank you," Jamie said, and hugged him good-bye.

After thanking Sam, Jamie headed home, and when she got to Steamboat Rock (that really does resemble a steamship), she flashed back to 1955, and their return trip from the dam—

—With her nose pressed against the window, a young Jamie stared up at the coulee wall. The excited radio announcer said, "Okay! Next up, the hit that flew up the chart to number one, AND is the theme song for the award-winning film with the same name. Who sings it, and what song is it?"

In stereo, Jamie's parents yelled, "The Four Aces— Love is a Many Splendored Thing!"

Jamie smiled, and looked out the window as they drove through the walls at the crest of the "Million Dollar Mile." "The book I write will be a hit," she said.

—In a flash, Jamie was back in the Buick driving through the same rock walls.

She hummed a few lines of "Love is a Many Splendored Thing," and then surprised herself by blurting out: "My book *will* be a hit!"

That night, Jamie opened the blinds just enough to see the cross. "Thank you, father, for not quitting on me. Please forgive me for quitting on you."

She fell asleep, knowing where she had to be at sunrise.

It was still dark as she set alarms for both kids, put out cereal, made sack lunches, and wrote a note saying she wouldn't be home until after dark.

Dressed in her standard attire, she and Rock headed out for the property. Rock yawned a few times, and although Jamie was overly tired, she knew she had to go.

Flames of pink, yellow and orange streaked over the silhouetted coulee wall. But within a short time, darkness gave way to light, the sky changed to pale blue, sunlight brightened the top of the wall, and springtime in the desert came into view.

Songbirds were out and about, probably finding breakfast for their young. Jamie hoped her own kids woke up in time to eat. But she couldn't worry about that. Not today. She headed for the house, but then in a second thought, walked towards the lake instead.

Halfway there, she couldn't take it, and fell to her knees in the sage. "FATHER . . . WHY WON'T YOU DO SOMETHING? I don't want to die."

Reeds and cattails surrounded the lake, like an act of resistance to the desert around it; and inside the living barricade, was a place of many languages.

Blackbirds that weren't all black, squawked in the reeds; a pair of Canada geese flew down from the shelf, loud ducks participated in lap swimming and hydroplaning, pigeons cooed from rock holes, and baby swallows peeped from mud condos built on the side of the cliff.

But there was another noise, one she couldn't peg. It sounded like electricity, but that didn't make sense— there were no power poles down by the lake. So *what is it? And where's it coming from?* No matter which direction she turned, the hum was the same; and the odd part was, it was both energizing and peaceful.

She sat down on a rock near the shore, and put her elbows on her knees.

"I don't want to die . . . but I am. And there's so much I wanted to do and see. I'll never see Luke's ranch. I'll never see my kids fall in love; I'll never see their babies. I'll never see the night sky from Kitt Peak, or hear a concert at the Acropolis—I won't even be here to soar when this book flies—how fair is that? It's not! And there's all the other stuff a dying parent and wife thinks about—of course I think about that . . . and this sounds absolutely crazy—but, Father . . . I still trust You."

And then a funny thing happened. After getting that off her chest and being honest with her heart, her spirit was lighter, her vision clearer, and she noticed every detail around her.

Two curious ravens hovered overhead, and as she got up and wandered close to the wall, they followed. Jamie knew the snakes were awake, but she also knew she was safe. Black-billed magpies flew out of the sage, and reminded her of those wooden whirligig birds that people stick in their yard for art.

She followed no particular path, and was surprised at how the coulee walls played with colors and shadows like a chameleon. Even the dirt surprised her: some was hard and cracked like Italian tile, some fine and soft like sifted flour, and some like a child's sandbox. Jamie bent down, scooped up a handful of sand, and let it fall through her fingers.

". . . To see a world in a grain of sand . . . ."

"Now where did that come from?" she asked her attentive dog.

She stood up, and continued walking. Rock took the opportunity to follow a scent he picked up, and darted off with his pencil tail twirling around like it was conducting a symphony.

The ground was a carpet of tiny wildflowers, and she bent down to pick a stem no larger than a straight pin. It amazed her that in something so small, God still made every detail perfect and complete.

". . . And a heaven in a wild flower . . . ."

Jamie sat down all the way, and pulled her knees up to her chest. "Where do I know this from?" she asked out loud, and then laughed when she spied Rock looking over the tops of sage to find her.

A row of ants marched by her boot, and as she focused in on them, she saw that the line of workers was almost six feet long, and ended up at a two-foot high mound of dried mulch that was being renovated.

"Boy, we could use help like this."

She stood up, dusted off her knees, and inhaled a mixture of mock orange and springtime sage. This reminded her why she loved to breathe.

Rock poked along with his tongue hanging out, so Jamie got the thermos from her backpack, and poured water in her hand. As Rock lapped it up, another line weaved through her head.

". . . Hold infinity in the palm of your hand . . ."

She knew somewhere in her memory banks, under all the cobwebs, was the reason she knew these lines; but she couldn't think of what it was.

They walked along the talus slope, which some call a "skirt" the way it flares out from the coulee wall. It contained rock small enough to support soil for grass, arrow leaf balsamroot, sage, and bushes of currant, serviceberry, and mock orange—of which she picked a branch.

"Now this is heavenly," she said to Rock, and held the white blossoms up to her nose. But there was something else along with the sweet, citrus scent. And it was coming from the air around her, not the branch.

I know this scent, but not from here—what is it?

She continued to breath in the woody, sweet-spiced air that was now thick like incense. Rock noticed it, too; so it wasn't a tumor-related heightened smell. She inhaled as much as her lungs could hold. And when she did, it was as if someone poured warm oil over her head, and she felt warmth clear to her toes.

She hadn't stood there long, she checked—the sun was in the same place. But it felt like an hour.

". . . And eternity in an hour."

Jamie was stumped. She couldn't remember why she knew these words, or what that scent was. She poked along, picking up rocks, trying to remember.

The day went by fast, and all too soon, the sun had moved to the west side of the coulee. Jamie didn't have much time, but there would be enough, if she hurried. She called Rock out of the crevice he was exploring, and they hustled to the mesa.

At the top, they sat side by side on the edge where Jamie had seen the Lord in her dream.

"Even though my heart hurts, I still trust Your plan."

Silence broke with a shrill, and then an echo. Jamie looked up to see the golden eagle appear from the top of the wall. It soared over the mesa, circled over her home, and then flew back over the top of the wall.

Jamie smiled, and looked across the canyon as colors began to change and a hush announced the day's end. "No, I won't be hearing a concert at the Acropolis; but I don't think anything could top this . . . and I won't be here when the book flies; but I *will* be soaring."

Rock licked her hand, and she hugged him before climbing back down. They walked back to the house as the sky changed from pink, to purple, to silver, and then to darkness.

Jamie put her backpack in the car, but had a feeling she should stay a little longer.

She gave Rock a drink of water and a cracker, leaned against the car, and mulled over the events of the day. Stars filled the night sky, and Jamie looked for the ones she knew: Big Dipper, Little Dipper, North Star—all present and accounted for.

"Thank You, Father, for giving me today."

At that moment, the North Star, and the stars in both dippers, moved out of alignment and formed a heart.

Jamie blinked a few times to be sure, and tears dripped down her face. "I love you, too," she whispered, as the stars moved back to their places.

"Rock, I doubt if you'd see that at Kitt Peak—no matter how big the telescope!"

Jamie pulled up to the little white house, and a scene from Sophomore English flashed through her mind; and then the lines made sense.

Her teacher had assigned an essay on the meaning of the first four lines of William Blake's famous poem, "Auguries of Innocence." At the time, it frustrated Jamie, and she handed in a paper that said, "How would a seventeen-year-old know about such things? Wouldn't a person have to experience life first?" Instead of the low grade she expected, the teacher gave her an "A," and replied, "Yes, an understanding of such things comes only with time."

Today she could write that paper.

Jamie *she* didn't expect a welcoming committee; but that's exactly what she got. Chris and Kayla were in the kitchen; *Happy Days* was on TV, and the aroma of pepperoni, dough, and tomato sauce filled the little house.

"Hi, Mom!" Kayla yelled.

"Sit down, we made you dinner," Chris said, bringing her a plate filled with pizza. "You look hungry, so we gave you three to start with."

Jamie dropped her backpack on the carpet and sat down on the sofa. Kayla came around the corner with a glass of pop, and set it down beside her.

"Hope you like root beer with your pizza; I know it's Dad's favorite."

"It's great . . . this is great. Thank you! But how did you buy everything?"

"Just enjoy it, Mom. I got paid today—so it's our treat."

"Yeah," Chris said, "and besides, we couldn't stand the thought of eating potatoes another day."

"You two are adorable . . . thank you."

Chris pushed Kayla back to the kitchen, and Jamie glanced at the TV. Richie and Potsie were sitting in the Cunningham living room, and Fonzie strutted in with his trademark "aaayyh!" and thumbs-up gesture.

Jamie knew that sometimes, it's the memories from the hardest times that end up meaning the most; and even though these weren't happy days at the Stemple home; someday, her family would look back and manage a few laughs—even if, at first, it was only to poke fun at the lovely lime decor, or spacious interior of their little house with a mouse problem.

"Uh . . . Mom? Earth to Mom!"

Jamie broke her stare, and looked up at Chris and Kayla, and then at her plate that was empty, and then at her lap that was holding three slices of pepperoni pizza—topping side down, of course.

"Well . . . at least I wasn't holding my pop."

After the kids went to bed, she reclaimed the typewriter from the garage, set it back on the desk, plugged it in and rolled down a sheet of paper.

So how do you write a book?

She stared at the white paper, and the daunting nature of the project took over. But then she took a deep breath, whispered, "one page at a time," placed her fingers on the keyboard, and typed:

CHAPTER ONE:

Teri hung up the phone and dashed for the door. She had no idea Paul was headed for a heart attack. He was always strong for his family, and now he was alone in a hospital, hooked up to monitors, cuffs, tubes, and a nitro headache thrown in as a bonus.

It was rush hour as Teri weaved in and out of traffic; and a soft, masculine voice helped her stay calm . . .

"The time has come . . . this is the way, walk in it."

Jamie turned out the lamp, knowing in her spirit that she had a role in something greater than herself, and for her it was boiled down to one thought:

It doesn't matter what I feel like . . . it matters what I know.

"Riley?"

"What?"

"Just making sure you're still with me."

Riley sat up straight, and stretched. "Wow! So that's how *Place of Sage* got started? Wow . . . ."

Kayla nodded in agreement, and knew that was only number one, in a lineup of questions, unless she could hit the pause button. So she pulled a left into the busy café and mini-mart.

"Riley, remember when we saw the movie *Smoke Signals*? Remember the Nevada truck stop? Right here!

Riley frowned, and checked out the location. "Right here? How do you know that?"

"Grandpa sent me clippings from the paper."

Riley looked about and said, "you know what's funny, Mom? That movie was about two people on a road trip, telling a story. Isn't that what we're doing? But I'm glad we're not on a bus! I like the title—two words. I think short titles are best, don't you? Like Grandma Jamie's title . . . *Place of Sage* . . . three little words . . . and about that book, I have a few questions. For starters, did Grandpa Luke really have a heart attack?"

Kayla turned off the engine for this one, and leaned back in the seat.

"Well . . . he left work in an ambulance, and was admitted for chest pains and an elevated heart rate. They kept him overnight, and released him the next day under three conditions: that he'd rest for a week, slow his life down, and continue to see the doctor. Well, the first part happened . . ."

Kayla looked out across the parking lot, and was quiet for a few minutes. But then, she sat up straight. "Riley, something just occurred to me."

"What's that?"

Kayla clamped her hands together. "There was something else about that day . . . Grandma told me that when she ran in the hospital, the volunteer at the information desk couldn't locate Grandpa, and since Grandma was upset, she started yelling. Well, this nice-looking orderly appeared, put his hand on her shoulder, and said, 'Walk with me, I'll help you find him.'"

"Okay . . . so that was nice."

"There's more—listen! So they walked down long corridors, and he made small talk to calm her down— you know, things like, 'How long have you guys been married?' How many kids do you have?' stuff like that— anyways, he walked her right to Grandpa's room.

"Yeah—that's great! That's what she wanted right?"

"Well yeah. Then Grandma shook his hand and said, 'thank you—you're an angel!' And *he said* . . ." Kayla paused to make sure she didn't blow the punch line.

"What? He said what?" Riley asked, an octave louder than usual.

"He looked at Grandma and said, 'Well now, that's kind of interesting.'"

"You're kidding! Was he blonde? Tall?"

Kayla shrugged her shoulders.

"Did he have an Australian accent?"

Kayla shrugged her shoulders again.

"Mom, he couldn't be—could he? Wow!"

They both shrugged, and stared at each other.

Finally, Kayla glanced at the time. "We have to get going—it's getting late!"

"Okay, but I want to see the little house."

"I figured you would."

Kayla took the first exit into Adalon, and the site of the grain elevators caused an unexpected feeling inside her, and she remembered when she first saw them. Back then she didn't realize their importance to the town.

They drove past the church with the cross, and Kayla thought Riley was going to jump in her lap.

"Mom! That's it! That's Grandma Jamie's cross, isn't it?"

"I thought you'd be scouting for that. So, Sherlock, if that's the cross, then where's the little house?"

Kayla was hoping for a longer suspense, but Riley pegged it immediately.

"There! That's the house—right there!"

Only in a small town could you drive down the road going under five miles per hour, and not be stared at, honked at, yelled at, or worse.

As they inched their way past the little house, a wave of memories crashed on Kayla. But she noticed something. Jamie was right. Those *were* hard times in that little place; but there was something special about seeing the house again. Maybe it was the years between then and now, she didn't know, but it was softer somehow.

Riley started laughing, and it took Kayla a moment to catch up.

"What? What's so funny?"

"You are, Mom!"

"Me—why?"

"It's pretty funny, that someone trying so hard to escape, would buy the same type of house . . . same color, same size . . . even our front yards are the same!"

"Oh, Riley that's just a coincidence."

"A coincidence! Okay . . . sure, Mom."

Kayla took a right on Main Street and cruised through the business district. At ten miles per hour, it took them just under two minutes to be back at the grain elevators. Kayla stopped the car and looked at a corner lot that resembled a small park—a nice lawn, a few good trees, and a wooden gazebo.

"I have to tell you a short story before we head out of town. And this lot right here is part of it."

Riley was all ears.

"You see, back in the late 1800's, Adalon's Grand Hotel sat here. And for one three-day stint, it housed a soon-to-be famous author, named Owen Wister. Now Mr. Wister wasn't pleased about his layover in our little town, so his view of the beauty around him was a little distorted. And this fact bothered your grandma. Anyways, his famous novel, The Virginian, set the standard for the entire western genre; and since its first publication in the early 1900's, there have been numerous reprints, movies, and a television series. But . . . the interesting thing here, on a local level, is that there are some who are convinced that Adalon is the real setting for the fictitious town of Medicine Bow."

"That's cool! So what was Grandma so bothered about—he was a writer, like her?"

"Exactly! But in doing a little research, she read a few negative comments—well actually, downright insults, he had made about Adalon and the Grand Coulee; and you can imagine Grandma's response. But then she read that he wasn't feeling well on his journey, and figured that was the reason he failed to see what was here."

"So . . . what did Grandma think after her research? Was Adalon the real Medicine Bow?"

"I don't know . . . she didn't get to finish."

"Oh . . . sorry, Mom."

Riley leaned back in the seat, and watched Kayla's expression. Kayla put both hands on the steering wheel, and took a deep breath.

"Well—you have officially toured the town! Now we better get on out to the ranch."

"So, Mom, do you realize that when you were talking about Owen Wister and the town, you said, 'our little town?'"

"No I didn't."

"You certainly did," Riley replied, with that smug look of hers; and then she remembered where she was with her questions. "Okay, so what about the ranch? They obviously didn't lose it or we wouldn't be headed out there."

Kayla had to smile at Riley; she had a style that wasn't quite her very own. And more and more on this trip, Kayla realized how much of it had belonged to Jamie.

"Uh . . . Mom? The ranch?"

"Uh . . . the ranch . . . it did start into foreclosure. And one day, this rich guy from California came to the little house, and said if he could move in on the weekend, then he would pay cash for the house . . . the little house! It was enough to cover the yearly payment and late charges on our land. Wild, huh? What a coincidence."

"Another coincidence . . . right. That's cool—so you got to move out to the property."

"Yeah . . . it's not like there was a third option. But the hard part, especially for Grandma and Grandpa, was that they still couldn't afford it, so it was still up for sale . . . and they didn't have money to finish the work on the house."

Kayla burst out laughing, and caught Riley completely off guard.

"Mom—what's so funny?

Kayla had to pull over she was laughing so hard.

"I'm missing the humor here, Mom. There's nothing funny about the ranch being up for sale."

"I know," Kayla said, trying to be serious. "But you have to picture this setting. The place is up for sale . . . and Grandma's living there. Can you imagine how irritated she was when people came out to look?"

"Well, yeah . . . I would be, too—so what's so funny?"

"Okay. First you have to remember, there were no phone lines out there—not for miles, meaning the realtors couldn't call first before showing up. So one day, a realtor in a fancy suit, knocked on the door, and said he was here with a couple from the coast who were looking for a great get-a-way place. Well, I figured Grandma would be mad, but instead, she agreed to it, and while the realtor went to get the couple, she opened the entry closet door, turned on the light, and said, 'now you be a good little widow, and greet our guests.'"

Riley's mouth dropped open. "No way! Grandma had a black widow in there?"

"Yep—she was saving it for the right occasion. And it worked great! The first thing the couple did was look in the closet and see a black widow—the size of a silver dollar—staring at them. Naturally they called Grandma over, and she casually looked up at the corner, and said, 'Oh don't worry! It's only the big ones that are deadly.'"

"Then what happened?"

"The usual. The lady ran out, the husband followed, the realtor glared at Grandma, and when they drove away, we had a great laugh."

"Mom, that's awful."

"I know . . . but it was fun! And it's not like she planted the spider there."

"Well, yeah, but she left it there."

"Only for the show, then she put it out."

"Put it out? She didn't kill it?"

"Riley . . . we're talking about a person who got an 'F' in biology because she refused to hurt a frog or any other living creature."

Riley smiled. "Boy, I had a cool Grandma."

"Yes, you did." Kayla stared at the gazebo, and was quiet for a moment. "And you have an extraordinary Grandpa. I don't think an ordinary man would make the sacrifices, and with such a good heart, the way your Grandpa Luke did."

Kayla started the engine, and turned the car around towards Camas Hill Road.

"And as those last years went from hard to harder, they were both amazing . . . but 1980 was the worst."

Chapter Thirteen

January 3, 1980

"Hey, Mom," Kayla said, putting away a box of tree lights, "I think we should agree, that no matter where we are, we all come home for Christmas. Don't you think that's a good idea?"

Afraid of what might happen if she tried to speak, Jamie just nodded in agreement.

"Kayla—catch," Chris said, tossing her a gold ornament.

"No—knock it off, you'll break another one."

That was the diversion Jamie needed, and she slipped away to her room. She locked the door, sat on her bed, and covered her mouth so they wouldn't hear her fall apart.

This was her last Christmas, and she knew it.

Chris knocked on the door. "Hey, Mom? Can I come in?"

"Uh . . . just a minute."

Jamie took a deep breath, and wiped away the tears. "What's up?"

"I almost forgot. We swung by Fred's today, and they had a few phone messages for you." He pulled three crumpled, pink slips from his pocket. "That's cool that they take messages for people who live here without phones. But, I'm sure they're wondering about you."

"Why?"

He unfolded the messages, but didn't hand them over.

"So . . . who's Evelyn? And what kind of a message is, 'Have you changed your mind regarding our discussion?'"

"It's nothing," Jamie said reaching for the slips.

"Well then, what's it about?"

Jamie tried not to look annoyed. "Just some headache medicine—who else called?"

"Uh, okay—what about this one from Sam. 'Have you seen the bobcat yet?'" Chris looked up. "*What* bobcat?"

"He said one lives on our land somewhere . . . now can I have the messages?"

"Have you seen it?"

"No," Jamie said, and grabbed the messages.

"Well . . . why is it such a big deal if you see it or not?"

"According to Sam, the bobcat is a 'keeper of secrets;' and to see him is to know the secret."

"Hmmp. What secret?"

"Uh, Chris . . . I think that's why it's called a se-cret."

"Hey, Mom . . ." Kayla said, walking in with the nativity scene, "I can't find the box this goes in—can I just pack it like this?"

"Sure . . . oh—wait, wrap it in a towel or something, so we don't lose the Magi."

"The *what?*" Chris asked with a frown.

"Magi—The Wise Men," Kayla said. "You know, the guys who brought Jesus gold, frankincense, and myrrh."

Chris still frowned, and looked at Jamie. "Why did they? I mean . . . I can understand the gold, but what's the deal with this other stuff?"

"Well . . . first of all" Jamie started, but then paused to choose words. "They wanted to honor God, and His Son, with the best they could; so they chose gifts that were rare and hard to come by. They gave their finest for Him, and He gave His finest for them—for us all."

"Okay . . . but what is frankincense?"

"Well, I looked it up . . . because I didn't know either. And from what I read, it's a gum that comes from slit-ting the bark of a tree that's found in places like Arabia and India. It has a woody fragrance, but at the same time it's spicy, sweet, and thick like—that's it . . . it was frankincense . . . the gift of the Magi . . . ."

"Uh, Mom? What are you talking about?"

Kayla piped up. "*The Gift of the Magi*—remem-ber—the play we went to about five years ago."

Chris shrugged.

"Come on, Chris, you remember . . . the husband
and wife had no money, and no gifts to give each other
at Christmas; so the young wife sold her beautiful long
hair to buy a chain for her husband's watch—which
was special because it had been his father's; and the
husband sold the watch to buy combs for his wife's
beautiful long hair. They gave up their finest for each
other: the true form of giving."

"That's real nice," Chris said, and left the room.

Kayla looked at Jamie who had sat back down on
the bed. "Mom? Are you okay? You have the weirdest
look on your face."

"I'm fine, Honey . . . thanks . . . ."

Before they knew it, it was February and freezing.
The kids' schedules were hectic, Jamie struggled to
work on the book, and Luke struggled to get home on
Fridays.

Another weekend went by, and at three-thirty Monday morning, Luke headed out to his truck. This time
he stopped before opening the door.

"I don't understand you, James. Why did you break
your promise? Why can't you get a normal job like
everybody else?"

"You mean like at a bank?"

"What's wrong with that?"

"Nothing, Luke."

She avoided his eyes; the confusion in them tore at
her heart. She wanted to turn down his coat collar, and
flip his soft hair like she use to, but she didn't. As he
drove up Hawkins Road, she leaned on the porch rail.

Please, Father, keep him safe for me . . . and help him to understand.

It was a teacher's in-service day, so for most of the day, kids were coming and going, and going and coming. Jamie spent most of the morning and afternoon hunched over her typewriter—but with very little progress. It was one of those days.

Chris and Scott burst in the house about four, and shortly after, Pink Floyd's "Dark Side of the Moon" album rocked the house. Jamie didn't pay much attention until the fourth song, "Time," came on.

"Is that a hint? Am I 'wasting the hours?'" Jamie asked out loud. "And what the heck does "fritter" mean?"

"I'm sorry, were you talking to me, Mrs. Stemple?" Scott asked, pouring a glass of Sunny "D."

"Uh—no . . . but how are you, Scott?"

"I'm good."

"Great . . . please tell Chris to turn that down . . . I'm trying to work."

A few minutes later, both boys dashed out of Chris' room. "Bye, Mom, we're heading out, see you at the game—and don't be late!"

After the door slammed, and Scott's car peeled out of the snow packed driveway, all was quiet. Rock looked up as Jamie took two pain pills with water, and then sat back down at the desk.

"I am going to finish this book," she said as Rock stared up at her.

She put her elbows on the desk, and rested her head on her wrists. "I don't know how . . . but I have to."

She closed her eyes, and Sam's words weaved through her mind.

"*. . . And no matter what, always give thanks for what He's given you. For the day will come, when you won't have to search for things to be thankful for.*"

Jamie got up and walked over to the glass doors. The white canyon was dotted with gold-tipped sage and bunches of tall grass, and the coulee walls reminded her of a swirled chocolate Bundt cake covered in white icing.

The longer she stared, the clearer the Master plan became. Minutes went by before she moved; and when she did, she got down on her knees.

"Thank you, Father, for *Place of Sage.*"

She sat back down, and the writing flowed.

Jamie arrived at the basketball game in time for the tip-off. Chris spotted her immediately and gave a low hand wave. She sat two rows up on the bleachers, as close to the door as she could, and was entertained by four young girls commenting on which boys were the cutest, and who looked the best in their uniform.

Jamie thought about how fast her kids grew up, and then, before she could stop herself, she started thinking about the things she wouldn't be there for.

Thankfully, the referee blew his whistle, and applause broke out across the gym. That helped to snap her out of it; and the boys were ahead 6–0.

But her head hurt, and she couldn't shake the dread that had come over her. Thoughts whirled through her mind, and Jamie couldn't tell if it was the seizure that was about to happen, or the demons that were trying to torment her. But whatever it was, it started out small:

"You're a fool, Jamie Stemple! Look what you've done—it's all a lie—"

But then it got closer, and louder, and soon it drowned out basketball shoes skidding down the court, and fans clapping and kicking the bleachers.

"YOU'RE A FOOL, JAMIE STEMPLE! LOOK WHAT YOU'VE DONE—

IT'S ALL A LIE—AND YOU'LL BE DEAD."

The seizure followed before she could escape. Jamie folded her arms across her chest, and prayed it would be short and unnoticeable. And it was, ending seconds after it began. It may have been the coldest month of the year, but her body felt like a human salt lick.

After the game, Jamie stuck around to congratulate the boys on their 52–39 win. And while she waited for the coach to finish his locker room speech, the snow fell heavy and fast. When the boys finally came out, Jamie talked to Chris and Scott, and then headed out alone for the long drive home—Adalon was forty miles away, and home was fifteen more after that.

Twelve miles later, she was caught in a whiteout. It was dark, snowing and everything was white—road—drop offs—wheat fields—they all looked the same.

"What am I doing out here?" Jamie yelled, ". . . alone . . . in the middle of nowhere . . . three hundred miles from Luke—maybe I am a fool—and what if there isn't time to finish this book—"she smacked the steering wheel with her fist. *Why didn't I leave when the other parents did?*

The truck came up fast and high, high enough that with its headlights she could see up ahead—and the four headlights coming right at her—in both lanes! There was nowhere to go; if she slammed on her brakes, the truck behind her would go right over the top of her!

But, in an instant—somehow—she watched the two cars go by. *But how?* The drop offs were at least eight feet, and this was a two-lane road.

And then He spoke. "There is time."

The semi truck pulled out around her, and from that point, she followed it all the way to the intersection of Camas Hill Road and Hawkins Road.

As she turned into her driveway, she exhaled a deep breath. "Thank you, Father."

On Monday morning, a solar eclipse occurred, delaying school until ten o'clock. Jamie, Chris, and Kayla enjoyed the event together, and then drove into town. After dropping the kids off, Jamie arrived at the post office promptly at ten. She was prepared for a box full of bills, but not for the news that came with it.

Milly Edwards died early this morning.

Jamie did what was normal after the initial shock, and thought back to her last time with Milly: They were here at the post office, both waiting in line for stamps. Milly said, "If you want the news of the day, just be at the post office at ten—on any given day—and you're always guaranteed more information than you bargained for."

How true that was.

Early spring marked Milly's memorial. Ice beards on the coulee walls started to drip; a "rat-a-tat-tat" on an old fence post announced the woodpecker's return; and on the lake, ducks scooped out small pools freed from the ice.

Jamie arrived in town early, knowing that nothing brings a small town together like a wedding or a funeral. She parked as close as she could to the Adalon Community Church, which put her about three blocks away. She wasn't surprised. Everyone knew Milly; and everyone loved her.

The brown brick church sat on the corner of the street, and reminded Jamie of medieval times. Beige indoor/outdoor carpeting ran up five steps to the entrance, and terra cotta planters filled with wood shavings, protected the bulbs that waited beneath.

Maximum capacity for the sanctuary was 150; it was filled to that, and then some. But no one concerned themselves, including the fire chief. They were all there to pay tribute to the woman who deserved to be "Adalon's Citizen of the Year" every year.

Jamie took a place near the back, and surveyed the altar. A large wooden cross on the back wall balanced the room, and below that the pulpit and short counters were full of floral arrangements from all over the country. At the end of the counter, on the right side, stood the American flag and a small organ. On the left, stood the Christian flag in white, burgundy and blue; and a piano, being played by her realtor, Erika Parks.

A montage of clips ran through Jamie's mind. She remembered Milly's bright smile and twinkling eyes as she said, "Welcome to Adalon," and handed her the loaf wrapped in cellophane and ribbon . . . when Chris led her out to the living room to see the Christmas tree standing in the corner . . . and Milly as she stood in the middle of the street and yelled, "Keep writing, Jamie!"

After a few minutes, the music stopped, and a silver-haired pastor stood up and cleared his throat. He proceeded to tell of a woman who measured her time the same way she measured flour for bread—with love. He smiled as he mentioned how many times he saw Milly walking down the street with a loaf of wrapped bread in hand.

Jamie looked at the filled church, at all the heads nodding in agreement, and wondered what it must have been like, to be such an integral part of a community.

"Milly had a gift," he said, "and she used it well. We should all glean a lesson from that."

Jamie looked up at the cross. Deep in her spirit, the impact of those words burned true. Like Milly, she knew her gift. But she also knew that the next memorial she was a part of, would be her own.

After the service, Jamie stared at the sign she had missed coming in. It was in a wooden frame, on a background of maroon and gold paper, and wrapped in gold ribbon. The letters were in black, and read:

"Jesus . . . The Greatest Gift."

Twenty minutes later, Jamie was in her house, and changed from basic black to jeans and a sweatshirt. She made a pot of strong coffee, and stood in front of the glass doors while it brewed.

Her thoughts were still at the service, so it took her a few minutes to realize, that what she thought she was seeing—was actually there.

The beautiful cat had reddish tan fur, and dark streaks on his legs that looked like rings as he walked on the lake. Halfway across, he stopped and looked up at the house. Jamie opened the glass door and walked out to the deck railing.

The bobcat turned to face her and sat down on the ice. *Was this for real?* Bobcats are nocturnal. People don't see them unless they want people to see them. And she knew he saw her. She read that they can easily see a feather fall to the ground, and a mouse darting through tall grass, so of course he saw her.

He didn't move. He just sat there staring up at her, like a silent sentinel; and she just stood there, staring at him. *So . . . you're my "keeper of secrets."*

After a time, he stood up and walked towards the portion that was thawing. From where she stood, Jamie could see the cracks in the ice, and he was headed right for them.

"No, go back!" she yelled, and was surprised when he stopped and looked up at her.

He extended his padded paw forward to feel the ice in front of him, and then around each side. *How did he know to do that?* Then he took a step backwards, and walked a safe distance around the cracks. After reaching the other side, he stopped and looked up at Jamie, before climbing up the shelf.

She watched the graceful cat scale the side of the wall; and in her spirit she knew: when Luke sees her "keeper of secrets," it's time to tell him she's dying.

A few weeks later, on a Saturday afternoon, the Adalon area was hit with the worst hail and windstorm in years.

After it ended, Luke and Jamie stood outside and stared at the roof. What three-tab shingles were left on the roof, were ripped, and packed with hail; and those that couldn't withstand the force, were scattered across the driveway, and hanging off the sage. There was no guessing what the weekend chore would be.

Since Kayla and Chris were gone, that left Luke and Jamie to dig in. For a while, Jamie was doing all right, and made quick work of picking up the scattered shingles. But then Luke needed her help on the roof. She slowly made her way up the ladder with a bag of roofing nails, and asked for help off the last rung.

"James, you've never been afraid of heights before."

"I know . . . I just don't feel so good today."

They patched half the roof, when a late model, black corvette turned into the driveway.

Glancing up, Luke said, "Who in their right mind would drive a sports car like that down eight miles of gravel?"

Jamie growled under her breath, and Rock growled from the foot of the ladder.

The car pulled up next to the house, and a scrawny man, wearing a brown polyester suit and sunglasses, jumped out.

"Wrong roofing material, huh? So how much?"

Luke frowned, and stood up—as much as he could after being on his hands and knees for hours.

"How much what?"

"How much land—and what do you want for it?"

"It's 280 acres, but you need to talk to our realtor. That is what we're paying her for."

"Nope. I don't like realtors—when's your listing up? It must be soon, you've had this place up for sale since you bought it." He looked around. "So what's wrong with it?"

"Nothing!" Jamie said.

The scrawny man glanced at Jamie, then dismissed her and looked back at Luke. "Two hundred and eighty, huh? You are going to landscape it, right?"

"Look," Luke snapped. "I'm busy. So, if you want any more information, go call the number on that sign."

"Man, for someone needing to sell, you've got the wrong attitude. It's a buyer's market out there—not a seller's." With that said, he growled at Rock, got in his fancy car and drove slowly down the driveway.

After the dust settled, Jamie said, "Yeah, he's someone I'd trust. And what would he know about roofing?"

"It *is* the wrong material for this area. But I didn't have any choice. I couldn't afford anything else."

So much for the day.

Half of Sunday was also spent on the roof, and the other half was spent on bills. So much for the week-end.

All too soon, it was another Monday morning, and Jamie watched Luke drive away again. *Please keep him safe, Father.*

She wrote for the next eight hours, and then headed for a much needed shower. But, when she turned on the faucet, nothing happened—no water—not even a drop. Same thing with the sink.

"Oh, no . . . not something else . . . I can't bother Luke," she said out loud. But what choice did she have. They couldn't go without water until Friday night, she didn't have a clue what to do, and she didn't have a close neighbor or friend to pop over and take a look at things.

She put it off for a few hours, trying to figure it out herself. But then she had no choice. She plunked on her ball cap and headed to Fred's to call Luke.

He gave her three possibilities to check on, and to call him back if nothing worked.

Nothing worked. But she couldn't bear to call him back, that wasn't fair to him—he was three hundred miles away. She didn't know what to do, so she did the only thing she could, and sat down to write.

It was about seven-thirty P.M. when Jamie heard a car pull up. *Good, the kids are home.* It struck her odd that she didn't hear music blaring, but she didn't give it much thought. She stayed seated at her desk, focused on the half-written page, and when the door opened, she yelled out, "Hi! How was school?"

"I didn't go to school," Luke said, and turned on the kitchen faucet. "Tell me when it starts running."

A few minutes later, water sputtered in the sink. It took a while to get air out of the lines, but after that she had her choice of hot, cold, warm—whatever she wanted.

Luke came back in and checked the bathroom sinks. Jamie didn't know what to say, except, "thank you."

"You should be fine now," he said and headed out the front door.

"Luke? Where are you going?"

"I have to get back. We're starting work early tomorrow."

Jamie looked at the clock. "But it's almost eight o'clock . . . you won't get back until midnight, and you're starting work at what—four? Why did you do this? You shouldn't have driven all the way over just for this."

"Of course I should've. I'm supposed to be the man of the house, remember? The man takes care of his family."

Jamie's eyes glossed over and her heart ached. Luke walked down the steps, got back in his truck, and headed out for another four-hour drive. Jamie sank down to the floor, and cried, "Please watch over him, Father . . . and please, let it be over soon."

By the end of April, they had replaced every section of the roof, at least once. It was the start of tourist season, and people were coming from the "coast" to buy recreational land and summer homes.

"People are just lazy," Luke said, as Erika explained to him the importance of curb appeal. "And you're not telling me anything I don't already know, but there's not much I can do about it right now. I can't even pay all the bills, how am I supposed to buy grass seed and plants?"

"I know," Erika said, as a white Cadillac turned in the driveway. "Okay, it's show time. These folks are from the real coast. Apparently, they're looking for a new summer place because the wife doesn't like the fog they get at the ocean."

Much to Jamie's dismay, they arrived at her favorite time of day. A breeze whipped up a few cirrus clouds to blend with pink hues, evening sounds were heard on the lake, and the air was warm, dry, and fragranced with mock orange and sage.

The older couple got out of the Caddy, and the lady exclaimed, "Oh, Harold, it's just perfect! Buy it for me."

Erika looked at Jamie, and said quickly, "Well, you haven't seen the inside?"

"Doesn't matter," the lady said, adjusting the wide scarf around her suit, "if I don't like it, we'll have it redone. Buy it, Harold."

The husband stepped up closer, and buttoned his suit. But before he could say anything, something caught his eye.

Down the coulee a billow of fog rolled in so fast—like steam on a window while taking a shower—and so thick, that it hid the lake, the coulee walls, anything that wasn't within two hundred feet.

"It's ruined!" the lady yelled, and stamped her foot. "I left Ocean Shores because of this—I wanted a view of the water, not fog. I hate fog! Good-bye—let's go, Harold."

The lady threw her scarf over her shoulder, and stomped back to the car. As they drove away, Luke stared at the fog, and Erika and Jamie looked at each other and tried not to laugh.

When Luke caught Jamie's smile, she said, "*What?* I didn't do anything."

"Oh yes you did—you jinxed this place." He shook his head, and went back to making a circle of rocks around the wellhead.

For the rest of the day, Luke was quiet.

Early Sunday morning, Luke packed his duffle bag, and headed out to the truck. He hadn't slept in the bedroom, so it took Jamie a few minutes to wake up and realize he was leaving. As the truck backed out, she ran down the steps after him.

"Luke! Stop!"

He rolled down the window.

"What are you doing?"

"What does it look like?" he said in a somber voice.

"But . . . it's only Sunday."

"James, I can't do this alone anymore." He shifted into drive and headed down the driveway.

Jamie didn't have the energy to move. She just stood in the driveway in her nightgown. "Please, Father . . . please bring him back to me."

It was one of those times when she didn't want to remember the "whys," of what was happening, she just wanted it to be over.

After a few hours of pacing, Jamie sat down with her journal and pen.

April 27, 1980:

I knew from the beginning, really I did. Somewhere, down deep, I knew what my choice had cost me. But still, I know it was the right choice. If it wasn't, I wouldn't be able to bear the pain. My insides are crawling, I want out of my skin, and everything in me screams, "Quit!" But then I look out my window.

Tears spilled on the page, and she had no idea what was taking place on I-90 in front of the exit for Sno-qualmie Falls.

Luke didn't have time to tune-up his truck, nor did he have money to pay someone else to do it; so he wasn't surprised when it started to choke, and then stalled.

He got out and slammed the door. "What did I do that was so bad?"

"Nothing that I know of."

Luke wheeled around to see a tall man with blond hair walking towards him.

"I didn't see you there," Luke said, and turned back to pop the hood.

"Well now, that's kind of interesting," the man said, with a distinct drawl.

"What is?" Luke asked, concentrating on the engine.

"The fact that you're thinking of giving up . . . and on your way to do so, your truck breaks down."

Luke frowned. "*What?* What are you talking about—and how would you know anyways?"

"Well . . . do you think maybe God is trying to tell you something?"

"*God?* He doesn't talk to me."

"Are you sure about that?" the man asked, pointing to the sign. "Look where you broke down. Wasn't it about twenty years ago, when two people took vows to love each—rich or poor—sickness, health—for as long as they both lived? And wasn't it those same two people who stopped by the falls . . . still in their wedding clothes . . . ring any bells?"

Luke frowned. "How do you know this?"

"First, why don't you slide in and give it a try; and I'll have a look under here."

Luke frowned, but what did he have to lose. He opened the door, and turned the key. It started right up.

"Well, thank you. But how did—?" Luke spun a complete circle, but the man was gone. He closed the hood, climbed in the truck, and stared at the sign.

Luke stayed in Seattle for the next three weeks. Springtime was the busiest in construction, and he was asked to stay and work the weekends. They needed the money, and it gave Luke time to think. And on the other side of the mountains, it gave Jamie time to write.

But, on the weekend of May 17th, Luke had a strange feeling he had to get home. So after making arrangements and packing his bag, he headed east, and pulled in around three o'clock Sunday morning.

Jamie didn't expect him, so there wasn't much food in the house. To be precise: one egg, a gulp of milk, a few carrots, an assortment of condiments, two potatoes, marshmallows, and a can of green beans. Not the right ingredients for Sunday brunch. So while Luke slept, Jamie took a shower, and then headed to Adalon for groceries.

She had slept in late, due to a rough night, so it was after eleven when she left; but since she had to pick up Chris from Scott's house at twelve-thirty, the trip would time out well.

Although . . . if she had listened to the morning news, she would have known . . . the eruption of Mount St. Helens began at eight twenty-seven A.M., and winds were carrying heavy concentrations of ash in a north-easterly direction towards Eastern Washington.

Luke brought his coffee out to the porch, and watched Kayla throw a stick for Rock. The ash came through the coulee in a dark black plume; forcing them inside, as it swept over, through, and around the house.

177

Jamie was on Camas Hill Road as visibility was cut by a quarter, and then by a half. She inched her way into town, and tried to figure out what kind of dust was fine like talcum powder.

Chris and Scott were at the hoop, and hurried back to Scott's house, half-joking about the end of the world.

Streetlights came on at noon, but did little good as the thick cloud of ash blocked the sun. By one-thirty it was black as midnight.

For the next nine hours, hot ash erupted from the crater, some of it traveling east over nine hundred miles. Adalon, falling in the three hundred mile bracket, received a blanket about an inch thick, not as bad as some towns, but worse than others.

Paper masks were worn to protect against the choking powder, and as the hours went by, Jamie and Chris worried about Luke and Kayla; and Luke and Kayla worried about Jamie and Chris.

On Monday, school was canceled; the fire department worked to clean the main streets in town; and the Stemples spent the day at home, just being a family.

The volcano had stopped modern life in its tracks, and given each person touched by it, an opportunity to put things into proper perspective.

Kayla knocked on the master bedroom door. "Hey, Mom, can I come in?"

There was no answer, so she waited a few seconds and knocked again.

"Yes? Come in!"

Kayla burst in the door, "Hi, Mom! Where's Dad—I wanted to ask—oops—sorry—I'll come back later." She spun around to leave.

"Kayla—you're fine," Luke said, propping up his pillow, "what's up?"

"Nothing that can't wait—see ya!" Kayla smiled, and backed herself out of the room.

Later that day, ash settled on everything in sight, and on most things out of sight. Jamie stood at the glass doors and wondered how the birds and animals fared . . . especially her bobcat and golden eagle.

"Well," she said, as Luke came out of the bedroom, and joined Kayla and Chris on the sofa, "there's only one thing to do at a time like this—marshmallow roast!"

Luke looked at the kids, and Chris said, "I know . . . she always gets like this."

"Come on, people, get on out here!" Jamie loaded up a wooden shish kebab stick with three marshmallows. "Remember, they're best when they're burnt."

Soon there were four sticks, and a total of twelve marshmallows hovered over the burner.

"What we need is a good rain," Luke said, staring out the window. "A hard one, like cats and dogs."

"Hey," Jamie piped up, "speaking of 'cats and dogs' did you know—Luke, you're on fire!"

Luke blew out the flames, and Chris rolled his eyes, "Oh, no—here she goes again."

"No, I was just going to say . . . that even though that's an expression; it is a fact that fish and frogs can fall out of the sky during severe storms—I'm not making this up! They get sucked up from lakes and ponds, carried off, and then later fall to the ground in rain."

Jamie pulled her stick out of the heat, blew out the flames, and started to eat the burnt layer. She looked at the tough crowd and added, "Can you imagine . . . go out for a hike, it starts raining, and you're hit by a falling fish!"

The three looked at her, and shook their heads.

After the marshmallows were gone, the kids left the room, and Jamie started the arduous task of cleaning ash off everything that wasn't vacuum-sealed.

Luke put his arms around her and said, "We're going to make it, James, I don't know how yet, but we will."

"I know," she said, looking at her dishcloth full of volcanic ash.

"And someday," Luke continued, "our grandkids are going to ask us, 'where were you when Mount St. Helens blew?'"

Jamie couldn't say a word, and turned to rinse out the cloth.

"James? Are you okay?"

"I'm fine . . . ."

Kayla burst out of her room. "Boy, I hope nothing else happens—graduation's in eight days!"

Jamie smiled the best she could. And Luke joked with Kayla.

"Yep. One down—one to go."

"Very funny, Dad," Kayla said, giving him a big hug.

The day of graduation arrived too soon. Seated in folding chairs, Luke, Jamie and Chris watched the gym fill up fast. Even on the best terms, this event was tough for parents, so when Jamie's smile turned to tears, no one paid much attention.

In step, and on cue, twenty-one graduating seniors made their way up to the stage.

Kayla was beautiful in her cap and gown, and Jamie smiled knowing what great lengths it took to pin the cap to her wild blond hair. Jamie was doing fine until she looked at Kayla's sandals, and as camera bulbs flashed, Jamie flashed back to their second day in Adalon, when a frantic Kayla ran in the garage looking for those wedge sandals.

Where did the time go?

Soon tears were dropping in her lap. But other than that, Jamie was making it through the ceremony without any noticeable symptoms.

But then, as the principal started handing out diplomas, Jamie's ears started to buzz. At first she thought it was the microphone—they were having a bit of trouble with it. But then she saw two stages, and twice as many students; and there was no time to slip out before her muscles started to twitch.

Luke looked at her hands as they shook, and grabbed them on instinct. Then he looked up at her face, and saw her pain. Since she was sitting on the aisle, he could only help from her left side, but he did so in such a manner as to not draw attention.

In one smooth movement, he held both her hands with his left hand, and put his right arm around her shoulders, bracing her against him, holding her tight until it ended.

At that moment, the principal said, "Kayla Stemple!" The room filled with applause, and Kayla walked to the podium and flipped her tassel to the right side of her cap.

On their way home, Jamie told Luke it was due to stress. But he didn't buy it. And she didn't like lying to him.

Luke left early the next morning, and then had to work through the weekend, so it would be the following weekend before he was home again. On one hand, they needed the money, and Jamie needed to write; but on the other, it felt like forever. But once Jamie knuckled down and focused on the last chapter of the book, and not on how bad she was feeling; time went fast.

In fact, the next two months sped by.

One hot July evening, Chris couldn't sleep, and peeked around the corner at Jamie. They both smiled.

"What are you doing up, Punkin? It's late."

"I can't sleep—I'm not orange—and I know it's late," Chris said, and grabbed the Sunny "D" from the fridge.

"Use a glass, please," Jamie said without looking up.

"Okay," Chris said, drinking straight from the carton. He pulled up a chair and sat down beside her. "One more month and school starts—why does summer go so fast?"

"Well . . . either you're having too much fun, or, maybe the earth rotates faster during the hot months."

"Uh . . . yeah . . . right, Mom. Where do you come up with this stuff?"

Jamie pulled him over for a hug. "You're growing up too fast—so knock it off, okay?"

"Oh, okay . . . so is this hug over yet?"

"Nope."

"Well, Mom, it's not like this is our last hug—we do this every day . . . I'll hug you again tomorrow—okay?"

Jamie let go of his neck, and tried not to think about what he just said.

"So . . . is Dad coming home tomorrow?"

"He'll be here."

"Good." He patted the top of her head. "Goodnight, Mom, love you."

"I love you, too . . . Punkin."

The next day, Jamie was up early as usual, and brewed a pot of strong coffee. She hummed a few bars of "Love is a Many Splendored Thing," and then stopped when she realized what she was humming, and what it meant. She walked over to the glass doors and knelt down.

"Thank you, Father, for *Place of Sage.* Thank you for making it a hit."

It was almost over, and she knew it. With the book almost done, there were only a few things left to do.

The following Saturday, Luke and Jamie were having toast and coffee in the living room, and Jamie got up for a second cup.

"James, did you write those two creditor letters I asked you for?"

She froze, and coffee spilled over her mug.

"Jamie—watch what you're doing!" Luke said, jumping up to grab a towel.

"Luke—I'm sorry . . . about the letters—I don't know what happened, I completely forgot."

"You've been doing that a lot lately. Even the kids have noticed."

Jamie glanced out the glass doors to avoid looking at him, and movement on top of the rock shelf caught her eye.

NO! Please don't let Luke see you. Go away!

She looked away quickly and watched Luke. For some reason, he felt compelled to walk over to the glass doors.

"I think I could look at this view for a hundred years and never get tired of it . . . it's like staring into a fire, don't you—James, come here—quick!"

Her heart clunked.

"It's a bobcat! Do you see him?"

Of course she saw him. And she knew what it meant that he saw him. But how was she going to tell him?

"I'm going to take a shower," she said, and hurried into the bedroom.

Luke stayed in the living room, and watched the bobcat. His reddish tan fur glistened in the morning sun, and he moved gracefully up the rocks, to the very top of the wall.

"Wow!" Luke shouted through the shower curtain. "How many people get to see *that* out their window?"

Jamie leaned against the shower wall, and covered her mouth.

"Too cool," Luke said, and left the room.

That afternoon, Luke was hauling dirt to the circle garden he made around the wellhead. Rock started barking, and he looked up to see Erika's white Pacer coming up the driveway. He wiped the sweat off his forehead, and leaned on the shovel.

Jamie looked out the window as Luke nodded to Erika, and two car doors opened. "Oh, great," she muttered, and quickly scooped up the pile of clothes she had just thrown on the table.

She met them at the front door, as Chris and Scott peeled up the driveway.

Ahh . . . the beauty of perfect timing.

Chris jumped out of the car, and exclaimed, "You should see the rattler the neighbors found on their porch this morning—it's almost five feet long! It has four rattles—and huge fangs!"

The young couple turned around and headed for the car.

"*What?* What'd I say?" Chris asked, with that sweet, little boy look.

Luke piped up. "Don't worry, we haven't seen a snake since we moved in."

Erika covered her mouth to keep from smiling, and knew better than to look at Jamie who said, "Okay—bye!" rather quickly.

Luke looked at Jamie and shook his head.

"*What?*" Jamie shrugged. "I didn't do anything."

Erika waved goodbye, and headed for her car.

Luke opened the front door. "You are not innocent, James."

"Come on, Luke, you know you want to keep it."

"It's not a matter of what I want. We don't have a choice."

Luke went in the house, and Jamie bent down and whispered to Rock, "He does . . . he just doesn't know it yet."

The evening weather was perfect for a canoe ride and a little fishing, so that's exactly what Luke and Jamie did. After serious prodding by Jamie.

On the stroll down to the lake, Jamie searched for yarrow in case of hungry mosquitoes. It took a while to find some, but her persistence paid off, and she held it up to Luke's nose.

"Wow—that's a strong-smelling plant—it'd keep me away. Where did you learn that girl scout trick?"

"Sam."

"Oh . . . your boyfriend."

"Very funny, Luke. But he is a true friend . . . and I'll be glad when you meet him—you'll like him . . . and he'll like you, too."

Luke paddled out to the middle, and they took in the view.

"It's like an airport out here," Jamie said, as the geese couple flew down from the wall, and three ducks took off in the direction of the house.

Luke smiled, and handed her the paddle so he could fish.

She had paddled half of the heart shape when she felt the onset of a seizure.

"Fish on!" Luke yelled, and started reeling in. "Hey, James, can you troll just a little bit faster?"

Normally, she would have laughed at his joke, seeing how she didn't have the paddle in the water. But not this time. And when it started, she knew it was going to be the worst so far.

It scared her, and Rock started barking from the shore. But it scared Luke more.

The large-mouth bass was ready for a fight, but Luke dropped the pole, and then tripped over it trying to get to Jamie; and before he could catch himself, both he and his pole were in the water with the fish.

Luke was afraid he'd flip the canoe if he tried to climb back in, so while Jamie struggled to get through the seizure, he pulled the canoe to shore as fast as he could swim, looking back at her with each stroke.

"James, don't move—I'll run home and get the truck!"

After they pulled up to the house, Luke jumped out and said, "I don't know what happened out there—but that's the second time I've seen you shake like that—and it scared me to death! I'm writing a note for the kids—and taking you to the hospital."

Jamie looked away, and after he ran in the house, she followed him, and continued on out to the deck. Her heart hurt so bad she thought she would die right there. Then she noticed the lake. It was black as night.

Luke ran out of their bedroom, and out to the porch. From the deck, she heard him yell for her.

When she didn't answer, he wheeled around, and saw her leaning against the deck rail. He wasn't surprised. He shook his head, grabbed an afghan off the sofa, and went out to get her.

Kayla came in the front door and saw her parents through the window. It amazed her: being eighteen, and knowing her parents were younger than she was, when they fell in love, and knew they were made for each other.

She watched Luke tighten the afghan around Jamie's shoulders, and was about to open the glass door when she stopped. Her parents were holding each other, and they were both crying.

The next day was unusually quiet. Chris and Kayla flipped pancakes and burnt the bacon. They kept looking at the time, and glancing at their parent's bedroom door.

"They never sleep in this late." Chris said, when breakfast was ready.

"I know," Kayla answered in a low voice, "something's gone wrong."

"What do you mean? They're finally getting along. Maybe they just stayed up too late—they are old, you know."

Luke came out of the bedroom. "Mornin.'"

Chris looked at the clock again. "Well yeah—for a few more minutes—it's ten to twelve!"

"Is Mom up?" Kayla asked, noticing his swollen, red eyes. "We made breakfast."

"Thanks . . . Mom will be out soon."

The kids looked at each other, and Chris piped up. "Dad . . . is everything okay?"

Just then Rock started barking, and Kayla looked out the window. "You know anyone in a black corvette?"

"No way," Luke said, staring at the driveway.

He shoved on his boots, and slammed the door behind him. Kayla and Chris glanced at each other, and followed him out to the porch.

"What do you want?" Luke said, to the scrawny man wearing another polyester suit.

"Have you got rid of your realtor yet? I can fit a lot of houses on a piece of dirt this size."

Luke looked at the ground, then back up at the man. "Just get in your car and get off my land."

The scrawny man put his hands on his hips. "You fool! Do you know who you're talking to? I'm the best offer you're going to get!"

Luke turned around and walked up the steps. The man stood there a moment, then got in his car, and peeled out in a dust plume.

"Nice job, Dad," Kayla said, and patted him on the shoulder.

Chris watched the corvette pull out of the driveway. "Why didn't you deck him, Dad? He was a jerk!"

"He doesn't matter," Luke said, and went in the house.

Later that day, Luke found Jamie sitting on a step on the front porch. "James, why don't you sit on the deck—a chair would be a lot more comfortable."

"I know . . . but I love the view from here."

"But from the deck you get to see rocks—and a lake!"

"I know . . . but I want to look at these rocks."

"It looks like a hat," Luke said, and bent down to kiss her, before disappearing in the house.

"But not just any hat," Jamie whispered to Rock.

A moment later, something hit the door, and Luke reappeared carrying a lounge chair heaped with pillows.

"There. Now you can watch your mesa in style." He helped Jamie up from the step, and propped pillows around her after she sat down in the chair.

"Luke, this really isn't necessary . . . but thank you."

"James, I'm going back to Seattle today—"

"*What?* Why?"

"Now hear me out. I need to make arrangements to have everything handled while I'm gone—"

"—Gone where?"

"I'm taking a leave of absence . . . so we can—I'm not going to just sit back and let this happen! We're going to fight this—I can't lose you, James—not after everything we—"

He couldn't finish. He put his head on her hands. "James, tell me this isn't really happening . . . please."

After an early dinner, Luke got in his truck, and headed out. After pulling out of the driveway, he noticed that someone had knocked over the realtor sign. He slammed on the brakes, jumped out of the truck, and put the sign back up. Then on impulse, he turned around and kicked the sign as hard as he could, causing it to buckle over.

Jamie stood on the porch and waved as he drove up the hill and around the corner. Watching Luke was all the incentive she needed. She got her keys, drove to the end of the driveway, pulled out the *For Sale* sign, and threw it in her trunk.

Enough is enough.

And then He spoke.

"It takes more faith to leave it up."

For a moment, she stood as still as the sign. Leaving it up went against everything she believed their land to be, and everything they had worked so hard for. But still, He was right. *Of course He's right—He's God!*

Jamie yanked the lopsided sign out of the trunk and stuck it back in the dirt. "There!"

She turned the car around, pulled back in the driveway, and stopped suddenly. She heard a loud hum—not the ring or buzz she was subject to—but a loud hum like electricity . . . and lots of it.

She looked down the driveway. Four rings of lightning were circling her house.

She knew her headaches could trigger flashes of light, but that's not what these were—she tested them—when she closed her eyes they were gone. So she stopped the car, and got out for a better look.

As she watched, the rings grew larger to encompass more of their land; and the bigger they grew, the louder the hum. This was pure energy, circling their land as far as she could see . . . around the mesa, around the lake, around their home.

She held her arms in the air, and watched until the rings disappeared.

"Thank you, Father, for this place."

Luke returned the following evening, and they hugged like it would be their last.

"James, I'll take you anywhere in the world . . . name it and we're there."

She was ready for this question and replied, "Okay, can we go tomorrow?"

"Well . . . that depends on where we're going, and what arrangements I need to make."

"Okay—I'll go pack."

Kayla and Chris waved goodbye, and assured them that they would be fine—Rock would get fed, and no, they wouldn't throw any wild parties.

For a time, they drove in silence; but then Luke rubbed his eyes, and said, "You should've told me sooner, James. I would've been there for you. I would've taken you around the world if you wanted to."

Jamie tried to smile. "I know . . . that's why I couldn't. That wouldn't have been fair to you."

"*Fair?* I don't care about that, James. I care about you! When we get home, I want a third—and fourth— opinion—I want to know what our options are—what we can do to fight this thing—I—"

"—Luke," Jamie grabbed his hand, "it's too late for that . . ."

"No! It can't be."

They parked in the busy lot, and walked around Douglas firs and picnic tables to get up to the lookout. They leaned against the rail, and for a moment, just stared. Snoqualmie Falls was exactly how they remembered it.

"I still think black and white are the best wedding colors, don't you?"

"Any color would be great on you, James."

Below them, on the river's edge, a young couple walked hand-in-hand, while two small kids threw rocks in the water. Luke and Jamie looked at each other, and knew they were both thinking the same thing: *How did the years go by so fast?*

From there, they followed the walkway sprinkled with Flowering cherry blossoms and a few early maple leaves; stopping to rest a few times along the way.

Neither wanted to leave, but when it was time they walked slowly back to the car, leaning on each other for support. Luke opened the door for Jamie and they both burst into tears.

They continued west to the ocean, and spent the night in a secluded cabin with sand and sea for their yard. There were things they had to talk about; but now was not the time. There were kites to be flown, tide pools to explore, and sand to be squished between toes.

At sunset, they curled up in a blanket; and laughed, cried, and remembered why they fell in love.

The next evening, Rock met them halfway down the driveway, his pencil tail working overtime. And when

Chris and Kayla came out to greet them, Luke grabbed Jamie's hand, and they both took a deep breath.

Jamie was sitting in her lounge chair on the front porch, when the black VW pulled up. The sight made her smile; as she knew this was the start for an important friendship. Luke came out, and she introduced Luke to Sam, and Sam to Luke.

After a solid handshake, Luke retrieved a third chair so they could all sit together, and then went inside to make snacks and cold drinks. But Jamie knew he was really giving her time with her friend. Sam and Jamie smiled at each other, and then stared at her mesa.

Sam knew that a dying person needs friends . . . and friends don't have to say anything—what *can* they say? They just need to be there.

The month of August passed quickly, as time always does when you don't want it to; and soon the sage was in full bloom.

Luke and Jamie spent most evenings viewing life from their front porch. They watched a farmer on the ridge end a long day in the field; and as the breeze blew in their direction, they heard his tractor chugging along.

"How is harvest this year, Luke, have you heard?"

"Yeah, it's a good one . . . finally. It's been rough on the farmers—last year the drought, two years ago the rain, this year the ash. But, I hear the Department of Natural Resources is testing the effects of ash on crops, so maybe farmers can use it to their advantage."

"I hope so," Jamie said. "But I feel sorry for the bees."

Luke's forehead crinkled. "The bees?"

"Yeah . . . I read that the ash took a big toll on insects, especially the bees. It literally dehydrated them."

"Only you, James, would worry about the bugs."

"Luke, look!"

They sat together in the lounge chair, and watched in silence as the full moon rose above the coulee wall and cast a glow across their land. Then, for an encore, a low flying dragonfly flew in front of them, and paused a moment to have a look; and naturally, Jamie reached out to touch it.

"I still say that's where the idea for helicopters came from."

Luke just smiled.

On the evening of September 2nd, and their twentieth wedding anniversary, Luke walked out on the porch, as Jamie wrote the last three lines of her entry:

". . . the first being greater than ours.
And in the first, the Master plans are made . . .
Place of Sage being one of them."

She closed the journal, and Luke carried her into the house.

The next day, Jamie convinced Luke to go fish awhile. She promised to sit on the deck so he could see her; and as he cast his line, she wrote an entry on the last page of her journal.

When she closed her journal of filled pages, she knew. The time had come.

Jamie covered her mouth, and stared at Luke. As if on cue, he looked up and waved at her. She waved back, and whispered, "I didn't break my promise, Luke . . . you'll see."

Rock winced as Jamie hugged him and told him to stay. She watched Luke cast, and then wave again. For the last time, she waved back.

Alone in the house, Jamie walked in Chris' room, and then in Kayla's, thanking God for His plan in their lives. But her heart couldn't handle much more.

She went in her room, and placed the original book manuscript—wrapped in a gold ribbon—on her pillow, under the covers. After smoothing the blankets, she walked out to the living room, and watched Luke as he rowed towards shore.

"He's a fine man. And I know you'll help him to understand."

Out of breath and shaking, Jamie made her way out the front door, and down the steps.

"Father . . . I still trust you."

In an instant, rainbow colors appeared from the mesa. But instead of arching to form a bow, they shot straight up to the clouds.

Jamie stumbled towards the mesa; and along with tears, she smiled.

Without looking up, she lifted her arm to touch his golden wing . . . .

How she got there, and where she was . . . she did know. It was splendid, and it was real . . . and she felt peace . . . such as never before . . . .

At that moment, the lake turned sapphire blue.

After watching a rainbow arch over their land, and not seeing Jamie on the deck, Luke rushed back to the house.

At the same time, Kayla raced up the driveway, and jumped out of the Buick in a dust plume. She waved a pink slip of paper, and shouted, "Dad—she did it! I picked up the phone messages—where's Mom? The book—it sold—it's a hit! And did you see that rainbow? It was huge!"

Chris and Scott were pulling in, and Kayla ran over to tell them the news. Luke looked at the house, and dropped his fishing gear.

"James!" he shouted, and ran up the stairs. "James!"

It was about five A.M., when the bottle slipped from his fingers and hit the fireplace hearth. Luke jumped.

"James?"

It took a moment for him to remember why his eyes burned so bad. "Oh, no," he screamed, and then covered his mouth so the kids wouldn't hear.

After stumbling to the bedroom, Luke crawled into bed, and out of habit turned to hold Jamie. "No . . . God, no . . . ." He reached for her pillow and touched the corner of her gift instead. Sitting up, he tried to dry his face, and then turned on the lamp.

The top page was reserved for the title: *Place of Sage*, and the second page caused a new flood of tears.

For the First author and creator of *Place of Sage*, and for Luke . . . the man who stayed when nothing made sense."

Tucked in the third page was Jamie's letter. Tears continued to roll down his face, and he tried hard not to cry out loud. Painful minutes went by, and finally, with an unsteady hand, he was able to read . . . .

Dear Luke,

Sometimes, something big comes along and takes our life by surprise . . . so it has been with our Place of Sage. All part of a Master plan.

The order of events will take time to understand. But that time will come.

And you were the hero, Luke—brave enough to commit to this plan, without the knowledge of why. And without you, this story would not exist.

But you must have felt like Noah did—building an ark in the desert with no sign of rain. These things don't make sense in our logical world. But I know in my heart, as it was worth it for Noah, it will also be for you . . . you'll see.

And the point is we did it . . . as God gave His finest gift for us; we, too, gave our finest. And because of this, His plans, for our children and grandchildren to come, have moved forward.

The rights to *Place of Sage* are yours. You'll know what to do with them when the time comes . . . and it will.

I love you always,
James

A month later, Luke was sitting on the front porch as Chris and Scott pulled up.

"How was school?"

"Fine. Come on, Dad, let's go fishing."

"Naah . . . you guys go ahead."

"Nope. Not without you. You've been sitting in that chair for weeks—come on . . . or are you afraid you'll get skunked?"

"No."

"Okay then, get up and get your pole," Chris said, yanking him out of the chair.

Luke walked slowly to the shed. His pole wasn't in the usual spot, so it took him a while to find it propped up in the corner, with a large box that read:

Luke—Do not open until you know where the barn goes!

He knelt down, and traced the letters with his finger. "Oh, James . . . what did you do?" He closed the door to the shed, rubbed his eyes, and opened the box.

Chris and Scott leaned on the car, and stared at the shed.

After a few long minutes, the door swung open. Luke came out wearing a dark brown Australian Outback hat, a long oilskin coat to match, and brown leather gloves. He strode past the boys, and pointed to the right side of the house. "Right there! The barn is going right there! And we need to get started—we've got a lot do before winter."

The boys were speechless as they watched Luke and Rock head for the mesa.

At the top, Luke and Rock stood by the memorial he had fashioned from a tall, flat rock. On it, he had etched her name, and below that positioned a vase for flowers. Rock sat close to the memorial, and winced.

"I know, Rock. I miss her, too."

He put new sage flowers in the vase, and rubbed the top of the stone. "Thank you, James."

All was quiet for a moment, and then Luke said, "Lord . . . if you're listening . . . is she with you? Is she happy? Please let me know."

He rubbed his eyes, and Rock leaned up against him.

And then, faint at first, and gradually getting louder and sweeter, they heard a flute. And they both heard it, because Rock looked at Luke, and Luke looked at Rock. As the music came closer, there was no mistaking the song . . . it was "Edelweiss."

Luke rubbed his eyes with the sleeve, and raised his hat in the air.

"Thank you," he whispered.

Chapter Fourteen

Kayla rubbed her face, and then looked over at Riley. "Well . . . now you know the whole story. And you were right . . . I did need to tell it. I've spent twenty years resenting it."

"But, Mom . . . don't you get the feeling it isn't over yet?"

Of course she did. The brewing she thought would be gone, wasn't.

Kayla made a right-hand turn onto Hawkins Road, and took the first corner a bit too fast. They looked at each other, and burst out laughing. It was easy to picture Jamie on that corner. But then, it was just plain easy to see Jamie on this land. The sage was blooming in shades of orange, yellow, pink and white; and Kayla remembered vases full of them in every room.

"Mom—look out!"

To avoid hitting the last two, of about fifty brown cows, Kayla slammed on the brakes, swerved to the right, and skidded to a stop with the front right wheel hanging over the embankment.

"Mom—do something!" Riley jumped away from her door, and sat close to Kayla.

The cowhand closest to them saw it happen, and rode over to help. The Indian man jumped off his horse, and leaned down to the window.

Both mother and daughter stared at him.

"Hi . . . are you okay?"

"Uh . . . I think if I throw it in reverse and gun it, we will be. But feel free to stick around, just in case."

"You bet," he said, positioning his dark brown Aussie hat.

Kayla took a deep breath, and changed gears.

"Uh . . . Mom?"

"Not now, Riley, I'm a little busy—hang on!" She stomped on the gas pedal, and within seconds they were back on all fours. Riley talked as fast as she could before the man came back over.

"Mom—that's one of the guys from the store—the younger one!"

He was about to lean down to the window, when the steer cut loose from the herd. He jumped back on his horse, pushed down his hat, and took off after it.

"They're bringing them off the ridge, so they must be rotating pastures," Kayla said, while keeping her eye on the handsome Indian.

"Yep . . . not bad for a city girl. He's pretty cute, huh?"

"*Who?*"

"Right, Mom! Like you didn't notice . . . hmm . . . remind you of any particular . . . *Snowy River* movie?"

"Very funny . . . ."

While they waited for the roadblocks to clear, Riley watched the cows, and Kayla stared out across the canyon.

Riley was about to comment on the cows, when she noticed Kayla's gaze.

"Hmm . . . there doesn't seem to be any half-dead trees here. Have you noticed that, Mom?"

It was one of those great mother-daughter moments, when nothing else needed to be said.

Then, on cue, the cows moved out of the way. Kayla turned in the driveway and drove through the black metal gate scrolled with the words: "Place of Sage."

Luke rushed from the barn to greet them, decked in his Aussie hat and jeans; and Riley couldn't get out of the car fast enough.

"Grandpa Luke!"

Kayla started to open her door, and then stopped. She looked close at the man who had said, "All right, James," to a crazy idea of moving his family over the mountains, to a speck of a town, in the middle of a wheat field. He was definitely the most handsome man she knew.

She got out of the car, inhaled the dry, desert air; and in true Kayla style, tripped over a rut in the driveway.

"Hi, Dad."

Luke held up his arms for a hug, and the breeze carried a chorus coming from the barn . . . .

". . . Love is when a grown man cries
he won't leave her side
it looks like we're in for a long, hard ride.
Love is when the Lord above
gave His only son
to wash away our sins . . .
I thought I always knew
I never even had a clue
now I know what true love is."

The moment was quiet as they both absorbed the words. Kayla looked at Luke, and Luke stared at the mesa—until he felt the silence.

"Well, we'd better get you unpacked, we've got a party to go to!"

But Kayla was still focused on the song. "That's Brooke Turner's break-out song. Like most great writing, it was written at a tough time in his life . . . but who's that singing?"

Just then, a man dressed in all black, including his cowboy hat; hustled out of the barn with a fishing pole in one hand, and tackle in the other. He waved the pole at Luke and headed for the lake. "The fish are calling my name!"

"Dad, that's . . . Naah, it couldn't be. So who was that?"

Luke just smiled. "Come on—let's get your things."

Kayla looked at Luke, and then at the man headed for the lake. . . *Naah*.

That night, crickets had competition as country music filtered through the canyon. Barn rafters wore streamers in sunset shades of purple and pink, tables were topped with white linen and sage flowers, and bails of hay placed along the back wall held trays of colorful dishes.

Kayla found a spot for the dreaded "dirt in little plastic skins," and Chris scooped her up for a hug.

"How's my little, big sister?

"Good . . . and what about our famous geologist? Wearing wranglers I see . . ."

"Don't start with me, Kayla, I'm still bigger than you! And Riley, how did you get so beautiful?"

"Hi, Uncle Chris," Riley said, as he leaned down for a hug. "Hey, I have a question for you."

Chris put his hands up. "Whatever it is—I didn't do it."

"No—it's nothing bad! Mom told me about a man you met on a basketball court."

"Yeah—I'll never forget that shot."

"Well . . . he said you would meet someone out here? Who was it?"

Chris smiled. "A geologist . . . from the Department of Natural Resources. He was out working on a land swap with the Bureau of Land Management. Yep, and from that day on, I knew what *I* wanted to be."

The band started up, Chris saw Scott walk in, Kayla spied the punch, and from across the barn, Riley saw the other man she'd seen at the store. But before she had time to find Kayla, he walked over to her.

"So what does it mean . . . to be Riley Stemple?"

Riley stood up straight and her eyes were big. "You're Sam!"

"That's me," he said, and held out his hand to her. "Your grandpa tells me you want to be an archaeologist—that's great! So let me know how I can help, okay?"

"That would be wonderful, Sam, thank you!" Riley stared at her grandma's friend. "Hey . . . you wouldn't happen to know anything about Whale Island, would you? I read a blurb on it while researching petroglyphs at Vantage—but it wasn't enough—I'm really curious about it."

"You're a lot like your grandma—I can tell already."

"Why thank you! I'll take that as a compliment."

"It is. And as far as Whale Island goes, I can show you pictures. I moved petroglyphs off that island, before it was submerged by the Priest Rapids Dam Project."

"Wow, I'd love that, Sam—when can we?"

From the punchbowl, Kayla heard Brooke Turner sing the first line of "Now I Know What True Love Is." She set down her cup, and found Luke in the corner with a distant look in his eye.

"May I have this dance?" she asked.

Luke turned and smiled, but Kayla saw his glossed blue eyes. *Mom was right; they are like sapphires.*

After Sam left for the hors d'oeuvre table, Riley scanned the barn for a familiar face. She caught sight of Luke and Kayla on the dance floor, as a tall man with blond hair came over and stood beside her.

"Your grandpa throws a great party."

"He sure does," she answered, still watching Luke and Kayla.

"He's a fine man, Riley."

Riley turned her head, and smiled. "I know . . . and I also know who you are . . . Mark."

Mark winked at her, and Riley beat him to his line:

"Well now, that's kind of interesting."

"It is—isn't it?" he answered, "but, Miss Riley . . . do you know who is dancing with your mom now?"

Riley turned towards the dance floor in time to see a tall Indian man, named Shep Andrews, tap Luke on the shoulder, and take Kayla's hand.

"I've seen him twice today, he—"Riley turned and Mark was gone.

At the end of the evening, the crowd whittled down to Luke's closest friends. He approached the microphone, and waited for the group to assemble on the dance floor.

Looking out at the faces, he smiled. There was Erika Parks, still striking with her long gray hair and turquoise jewelry; Sam, who'd become as much of a friend to Luke, as he had been to Jamie; Sam's son, Shep, who Luke knew they'd be seeing a lot more of, and not just because he liked to help with the herd; Riley, who was becoming more like Jamie every day; Chris, who found his way, just like they knew he would; Scott, who was still one of the family; and Kayla, who very soon, would realize how dreams come true. And . . . in the very back of the room, stood the tall man with blond hair, who long ago, was sent to help them along the way.

"Thank you—all of you—for being here. Today—September 2, 2000, would have been our fortieth wedding anniversary. I wish you all could have known Jamie the way I did. She had this way of seeing things, long before they made sense. It took me a while to understand. But now that I do, I'd like to share a thought with you."

Kayla's heart clunked when she realized the book Luke opened, was Jamie's worn black journal.

"It's her last entry, she wrote it the day she died. And if you've ever wondered about Jamie and this land . . . well . . . ."

Luke cleared his throat and took a deep breath.

"September 3, 1980:

It is here, in this place of sage perfume, where the pain finds its place, and my soul finds peace.

It is here, because God is here.

And even though you don't have to climb a mesa to talk with Him, it sure is nice to be able to."

Luke looked down, and then waved. "I love you all—thanks for coming."

Early the next morning, Kayla found Luke sitting on the front porch.

"Hi, Dad, may I join you?"

"You bet. I've been waiting for you to get up." He gave her a hug, and continued. "Do you remember what I asked you before you left Seattle?"

Kayla knew, but said instead, "To bring the lima beans?"

"Well, that, too—they were great by the way, thanks."

Kayla crinkled her nose, and waited for what he would say next.

"I asked what you wanted to be when you grew up."

"I know, Dad, but—"

Before she could finish, Luke jumped up and disappeared in the house. Kayla sipped her coffee, and stared up at the mesa. The air was fragranced with sage, and a warm breeze lifted sounds of birds and rustling grass through the canyon. But, there was another sound, and if it weren't crazy, she'd swear it was a flute. She gripped the handrail as the brewing inside her welled clear up to her face.

Luke came back out with two books, and placed them in her hands.

"It's time you make a film . . . don't you think?"

Kayla looked down at the books. One was *Place of Sage*, and the other was Jamie's journal. She couldn't speak. She looked up at Luke; he couldn't either.

"Good Morning!" Riley said, and burst through the door. "Is anybody else starving?"

Luke smiled at Kayla, and walked over to hug Riley. "Come on—how about you and me making breakfast?"

"Yeah," Riley said as they went in the house.

Luke paused by the window, as Kayla walked towards the mesa.

"Grandpa Luke, look at the lake—it's as blue as your eyes!"

At the top of the mesa, Kayla found two memorials, side by side. The second stone was smaller, but the same sculptured shape, resembling a shield.

"Oh, Rock . . . you were the best," Kayla said, and added more sage flowers below his etched name.

At Jamie's memorial, she set her flowers by the vase already overflowing with color.

"I miss you, Mom."

She sat down by the stone, and opened the journal. A small envelope slipped out, and when she saw her name scrolled on the front, her heart twisted clockwise.

Careful not to tear the paper, she opened the envelope, and read the letter inside.

Dear Kayla, my filmmaker,

How did I know God has great things in store for you?

It started with a plan. He put it in your heart and wrapped it with your dreams.

But He didn't just put it there, and then leave. No, he stayed to help you unwrap it. Listen with your heart, Kayla . . . He's there.

The place, the book, your film . . . it's all about a Master plan. And I know you're ready.

Never forget how much I love you.

Love Always,
Mom

She closed her eyes; and down deep, in that place where the heart and mind connect; there was no denying His soft voice in her right ear.

"The time has come . . . the story is yours."

Kayla stood, and held the books up high. "Thank you . . . now I know."

It's all about a Master plan . . .
Are you ready for yours?

To order additional copies of

Place of

Sage

Please call
1-877-421-READ (7323)

or visit our web site at
www.pleasantword.com

Visit Lyn on the web at: www.lyndnielsen.com

Also available at:
www.amazon.com
and
www.barnesandnoble.com

LaVergne, TN USA
28 December 2010

210296LV00002B/1/A